Dick Price

in

Big Sur

Dick Price in Big Sur

by John Francis Callahan for The Gestal Legacy Project

Copyright © 2019

ISBN: 978-0-359-21415-0

*All rights reserved. For private use only.
Not to be reproduced for profitable use or distribution. Do not publish or sell in any form, by itself or as part of another work, without express written permission.*

This is a work of speculative historical fiction. It is based upon creative imagination. All the characters and events are fictional and not intended to be consistent with consensual reality.

We sit together, the mountain and me,
until only the mountain remains.

Alone
Looking at the Mountain
--Li Po

What about you? Where are you? What are you doing?

Wherever you are is here. Whatever you're doing is now.

Thinking... That's mostly what you do. Especially when you're reading.

So take a moment... Wherever you are. Whatever you're doing. And take a breath.

Go ahead. Right now. Just breathe. Take a breath and feel whatever you're feeling. That's what you have right now ... really.

You're in a body. So have that experience while you can. Right now. Right here. Breathe and feel whatever you're feeling. Even if you don't read any more of this. You'll have that much. Give that much to yourself while you can.

That was my teaching. That was my practice.

I was Seymour Carter. Now I'm dead. Time and space collapsed for me.

I was wrong about death. I thought it was the end. I was going to die and that would be it... Oblivion... But I was wrong. Looking back at death now, I could have figured it out.

You drop the body and there's still awareness. Assuming there's awareness before, which is what I taught, there's awareness after.

I died in the Ukraine, at a friend's house in the town of Chernivtsi, in the year 2012. I had a heart attack in the bathroom. Several years before that I had a heart attack sitting in my car, back home in Big Sur, California. Ronnie Hare found me. He was driving up the road at Hurricane Point. He spotted me at the turnout looking over the Pacific Ocean, sitting in the driver's seat hunched over the steering wheel, looking like the worst kind of purple trouble.

Later on, Ronnie killed himself at Esalen Institute, sitting in his pickup truck – windows rolled up, the exhaust rigged to blow in.

That was my first heart attack. Back then I thought I was dying. The second heart attack did me in. I had been invited to do a Gestalt therapy workshop at the Moscow Gestalt Institute. Then another workshop in Kiev. There was a revival of Gestalt going on in Europe. I had lived in Germany for several years, on sabbatical from Esalen. So I was encouraged by the invitation. Revolution was in the air in the Ukraine, just like Berkeley back in the Sixties. There was renewed interest in my work. I ate it up. At last, I hoped for a humanistic revival.

Except ... then I died.

I had been part of a group of practitioners who revolutionized psychotherapy in the 1960s and 1970s at Esalen Institute. We were students of Fritz Perls and his Gestalt therapy. The undisputed leader of our group was Dick Price, the co-founder of Esalen. Dick transformed therapy into what he called Gestalt Practice. But now I'm dead. And Dick died before me in 1985, struck in the head by a boulder while he was working on the Esalen water supply back up Hot Springs Canyon. Dick's death was the beginning of the end of the human potentials movement, even though many of us carried on his work. Then, after the Millennium, there was new interest. That's why I want to tell the story of Dick's life and death.

I'm telling this story from a different kind of place. When I died my awareness started to separate from the material world.

Floating up like a blimp or one of those multicolored hot air balloons that rise up in the early morning chill from fields in Napa Valley to watch the vineyards quietly retreat below. That's what it felt like. That's what I was aware of.

Most of the work that we did in therapy involved body centered awareness. But my awareness separated from my body when I died, rising up out of that bathroom in the Ukraine. And I found out how it works.

It's possible for a body to exist without any awareness – like a zombie. But the main idea of practice is to wake up. That's what the Buddha was talking about. After the Buddha got enlightened he was walking along a road… Somebody saw him coming and asked him, "What are you? Some kind of God?"

He just said, "I am awake."

Of course, there's that other saying that goes, "If you meet the Buddha on the road, kill him." Which I suppose gets us back to the main point.

I'm in this place... Awareness space... Gradually, awareness fades into the background of the Cosmos – the big awareness. But for a while the pattern of who we are resonates on, until we get synced-up with the whole thing. Some of Dick is still here, but not for long. He's moving out. Still, it helps to be in touch with him so I can tell this story. He can see everything and anything – the whole panorama.

Now Dick understands even more and he helps me to understand. He shows me the big picture – how humans are a stage in the process of expanding awareness. How there are just a few more generations of humans left. ...That we are like Neanderthals. We fail as a species in the long run, but we are a bridge to another kind of being with a form of consciousness beyond human. Their consciousness will transcend time. That's what our work was all about. That's what we were in touch with, working to expand awareness. With Dick's help I can see the broad expanse – and that's what I'm doing. Telling Dick's story and the story of the arc of the Cosmos.

Dick helps me to understand that the story began long before our lives. It really began even before Big Sur. Dick helps me see his past life in Big Sur when we humans were at our best, before the decline started. So really, there was no decline, because what comes after us is always already there.

Dick tells me, *"There were many generations in Big Sur. Like the ocean. Many many generations of humans before the first Europeans showed up. My father was a Shaman living on what you and I later called the Peninsula of San Francisco. He was of the Yelamu tribe, of the Ohlone people – the Coastanoan Indians who came down from the north. My father lived on a hill overlooking the big bay to the east. And he had a camp on the beach to the north, looking across the straight that opened out to the ocean. Across that straight was the holy mountain named* támal pájiṣ *in the Coast Miwok language – what we later called Tamalpais.*

My father taught me how to live with the Earth in this place. He took me to the ocean and taught me how to gather food. He took me to the forest and taught me how to hunt. He showed me how to gather acorns and berries and seeds and herbs from the ground. He taught me the ways of a Shaman – how to heal. He taught me how to make a sweat lodge, to smoke herb and to carefully prepare the seed of the toloache flower that helped us see the Nine."

Dick explained to me how his father followed the Kuksu Nine – the spirit guides of the north, where the original Ohlone came from. Kuksu was the "big head" – the coyote avatar for the nine spirits of the world that came with the hummingbird and the eagle. Later on, in our time, Dick believed that the Nine came from the star Sirius. Now, in this awareness space, we can see that the mind of the Nine comes from a species that will replace humans – a consciousness that emanates from the future. We all could feel that, imperfectly, in our time – and it guided us as we worked with our awareness.

Dick explained to me, *"When I was ready, as a young man, my father sent me south to start a new tribe. He gave me nine pieces of black glass stone that came from the northern mountains, the eye of the Nine. These were precious pieces of what later on we called obsidian – with sharp edges that would cut like a knife, and just as useful for healing. I took the stones and packed them with some food to carry with me on the trek south. And I left my father's tribe to start a new life."*

Dick told me how he made his way along the coast. The trails were good down the Peninsula – easy hiking through the spine of hills, passing through redwood forest. He camped in a valley next to a long freshwater lake. Then the next day, moving out to the coast, he came to a wide bay like an open dish facing out toward the ocean and he camped for the night on the broad sandy beach. Starting out the next morning he hiked along the shore of that bay, moving inland to cross a river, then down toward the end of the bay and onto a peninsula that much later the Spanish would call Monterey. This was home to the Achasta tribe of the Ohlone. Dick found the tribal elder and made peace with him by smoking herb and making a gift – one of the pieces of black glass. He stayed many days with the tribe, making friends by practicing his Shaman ways, curing aliments, healing wounds and using herbs on infections, ringworm and rashes.

And he talked about the land to the south – the place he wanted to settle. Finally the time came for him to move. He set up a trade with the elder. He would give seven pieces of the black glass, and in return he would take four women from the tribe with him. They each had given birth and were fertile. They could cook and gather food and they had good dispositions. Dick knew that these women would actually start the tribe. He would be their partner and helper. So he carried along an assortment of stone tools for chopping and grinding, and several good deer skins for cover and shelter.

The trail south did not go far. It ended where the coast turned wild and rugged. There were cliffs along the ocean, rising up abruptly from the ocean. Valleys and ravines cut into the mountains, filled with dense stands of ancient redwood trees. This was not unexpected. This was the land where Dick had been sent by the Nine. After a long day of hard travel they came to a little river in a steep ravine with a mountain behind capped by white rock, as if it had been touched by the Nine. Then they came to a flat plain with a long beach. There was a large outcropping of stone on the coast at the far end of the beach. Dick knew this was the beginning of his tribal territory. He called it "the rock." ...In his language, he said: "Xue elo xonia eune" – "I come from the rock." ...He took his name to be Ex'selen and he told the women that their tribe would be called the Esselen.

They moved on south. The going got very hard – no trails. Dick, now Ex'selen, and the women crossed the wide mouth of a river that came down from a broad valley. Past the valley they came to steep cliffs. Climbing upward, they had to bushwhack through thick chaparral on slopes high above the ocean. Ravines cut down toward the ocean and they had to cross fast moving creeks flowing down from the long coastal ridge thousands of feet high. It took two more days for them to find the place that Dick had heard of – a place known as "the coming together of three waters."

There was a creek coming down through a canyon, flowing down from a spring high up the ridge, with a gushing waterfall emptying into a rocky ocean inlet. And there were hot springs with sulfurous water that gathered into a pool on a broad ledge of open land over the ocean. This would be the home of the Esselen tribe. Dick and the women built a permanent campsite – a hut shelter of timber covered with fir branches – on a flat space back up the canyon. Dick told me about what they did next:

"We made a life for ourselves. We built a steep path down the cliff to the ocean where we went about gathering shellfish. The shallows were rich in abalone, mussels and limpet. That summer we had plenty to eat from the sea. Then, in the early fall, we cut a path back north a long way to a cove that opened back into a broad canyon that was dense with a stand of black oak and tan oak, and we built a campsite there. That fall the oak trees dropped hundreds of acorns – more than we could ever collect. We gathered them during the day and in the evening we sat around a fire and cracked open the acorn shells and put the nut-meats into deer skin sacks. Then we carried our harvest back down the path to our Esselen home where we ground the pulp on flat rocks with hand-held stones and soaked

the meal with creek water to take out the bitterness. From this we made acorn porridge, or ground the meal to make flour that we baked to make bread. Rain came late in the fall, and with the rain there was a bloom of flowers and herbs, as if spring came right before winter. The days grew short and cold. We would eat a dinner of abalone steak and acorn bread. Then at night we would settle into the pool of hot spring water and look up into the black blanket of sky, filled with stars like spirits in the sky, and listen to the ocean pounding against the cliffs, and our hearts and minds opened to the Nine."

A few stray Indians lived back in the mountains. They didn't have a tribe – just a few stragglers who wandered south. Gradually, they came to Dick's camp at the three waters. Dick cared for them as best he could. They were hungry or they suffered from illness. Dick fed them and healed them. By the time winter came, a half-dozen of these stray people settled into the hot springs canyon, and Dick had the makings of a tribe. Before the end of first year, two of the women gave birth to sons. Dick built a sweat lodge by the waterfall and made a ceremony to honor the first born souls of the Esselen tribe.

The next summer Dick built two more camps.

"We worked for many days to cut a long trail south, down to a big creek that reached back into the mountains. When we finished, it was a day's walk down the path, so we built a permanent campsite in the forest up that creek. The water was rich in trout. We cut spears from willow branches and speared the fish. In some places the trout were so crowded together in the water that we could just grab them with our bare hands. We cleaned the fish and then built a tented fire to smoke them. When we had a load of smoked fish we carried them back to the Esselen home.

"Later we decided to build another trail north – back up to the Ex'selen rock – to the rock that gave its name to me and our tribe. First, we worked uphill from the three waters – up the ridge to the crest, where the ridge ran north and south along the coast, and we worked our way north so the trail would avoid most of the roughest canyons close to the ocean. At the

end of the ridge there was a long canyon with sycamore trees that led down to a beach. Here we built a large campsite. And from here we could hike back into the valley that held that big river we had crossed on our way down south from the rock.

"The river was full of trout and the valley was full of wildlife that we could hunt for food. There were herds of deer. I hunted them by covering myself with a fresh deer skin... I would carefully move into a herd, carrying a sharpened spear made from a sycamore branch. When a deer came close to me I would shove the spear into its heart to kill it. Then I carried it back to the sycamore canyon. That night we would have a sweat lodge to honor the deer and purify the killing. Then we would butcher the deer and carry the meat with us, along the trail back to the Esselen home camp."

Dick told me how, as the years passed, the Esselen tribe grew in size. They learned to honor and make peace with their neighbors – the mountain lion and grizzly bear. They learned how to trap rabbits on the land and otters in the sea. The tribe moved between campsites to harvest food. Other camps were built along the coast and into the mountains. But the tribe would always come back to the Esselen home-site of the three waters, where Dick was Shaman.

Every year Dick made a pilgrimage to a mountain top in order to thank the Nine. It was the tallest mountain at the southern end of the coast ridge – a cone-shaped peak that shot upward five thousand feet above the ocean. In order to get there Dick had to climb back up the hot springs canyon to the crest of the ridge, then work his way south along the crest, and then climb the peak where he could see the entire coastline and back across the mountains east into the interior valley. From that peak he could see like a condor, watching the whole range of mountains spread out below. He brought herbs with him that he would chew through the night, and the Nine would come to see him from the stars.

After many years, the Ex'selen Shaman – Dick – he wasn't really old but he wasn't young anymore – and he felt something coming. He knew it was time to make a final trek to the cone peak. He was gone five days – too long, it seemed. The tribe people got worried and sent two men up along the ridge trail in search of him. They found Dick's body where he had been climbing. He had been struck by a rock fallen down off the peak – and killed. The men carried Dick back to the Esselen campsite. His body was washed in the hot springs pool and wrapped in deer skin.

"They buried me in a hole dug into the cliff, facing the ocean and the setting sun. They put the ninth piece of black glass from my father in the palm of my right hand so the Nine would stay there with me."

Despite Dick's death, the Esselen tribe lived on and flourished as part of the natural world. Their home place became the center for awareness of the Nine, between the big river and the rock to the north, down to the big creek and cone peak to the south. As the years passed the collective consciousness of the tribe grew. This was the peak of human development. Perhaps, if they had been allowed to develop in peace, the Esselen might have evolved directly into the Nine.

But that wasn't to be the path of the human trajectory – not the path we would take.

Humans took a wrong turn. Europeans invaded and brought destruction. The Spanish came up from the south – up from San Diego. Spanish Catholic missionaries arrived in the new colonial capital of Monterey in 1770. At first they weren't able to penetrate the coastal region to the south that they called "el pais grande del sur" or simply "el sur grande" – the home of the Esselen.

These Spaniards smelled bad to the Indians. They didn't have very good personal hygiene. They didn't care about the damage they did to the natural world. The Spanish were deceptive and violent. Spanish missionaries set up monasteries – one in Carmel, just north of mountains, and one in the valley east of the mountains, under the tallest peak they named after their leader – the one they called Padre Junipero Serra.

The missionaries lured some of the Indians with beads and junk trinkets – the Esselen were introduced to con-artists for the first time. Then the missionaries sent Spanish soldiers into the mountains – mountains they called the Santa Lucia – in order to round up more Esselen by force. In the name of religion they put the Indians to work at farming. But the crops were poor and the Esselen were cut off from their natural food. They started to catch diseases from the missionaries – syphilis, measles, smallpox – because the Indians had no immunity. Spanish imprisoned and tortured the Esselen or used them for sex or slavery. If one or more would escape from the monasteries – running back into the Santa Lucia Mountains – Spanish soldiers would be sent to capture or murder them. Under the domination of Catholic missionaries the Esselen slowly but surely died off. After a couple of generations they were mostly gone, and the few who remained – estranged from the Nine – groveled toward extinction under the sick European cult of death.

Mexico seceded from Spain in 1822 and the character of European presence in Big Sur changed. Mexico expropriated mission property and distributed some of the land to private ranchers. There was a genuine attempt at economic development along the coast. The Mexican government made two huge land grants for rancheros of almost 9000 acres each. The first ranchero starting just south of the Carmel Mission ran down to the Little Sur River, which was one of the rivers that Dick, as Ex'selen, and his wives had to cross to reach their tribal land. The second ranch, named Rancho El Sur, went from there all the way to the mouth of the Big Sur River including Point Sur or "the rock" of the Esselen, but not quite as far as the tribe's Sycamore Canyon camp. Of course the Esselen were long gone. Instead of Indians, the Mexican rancheros mostly exploited non-native animals like cattle and pigs. A few remaining Indians where converted into cowboys or ranch hands.

Then there was the Mexican War. Big Sur became part of the United States in 1848 and California became a state in 1850. With statehood came a huge influx of Americans along with the California gold rush. American settlers appeared in Big Sur starting in the 1860s, homesteading claims of 160 acres for each family member. There were families that became iconic in Big Sur – a French family named Pfeiffer (they pronounced it "Piefair") and the Post family. The Pfeiffers settled in Sycamore Canyon. The Posts along the Big Sur River. Far south, close to Big Creek and Cone Peak, the Harlan family grew into a small community, later called Lucia. But there was little connection between the Harlans in the south and the Pfeiffers and Posts in the north. The rugged pattern of cliffs and canyons that Mexicans had called *La Baranca* made travel difficult. There was only a rugged wagon road from Monterey down to the Rancho El Sur, but for the next thirty miles there was nothing better than risky horse trails.

One important settlement for our story was started by a man named Thomas Slate. He discovered the hot springs at the old Esselen campground. Soaking in the hot sulfur water was good for his arthritis. So he decided that the place might attract tourists – might even become a hot springs resort. Slate filed a homestead claim in 1882. But ultimately he couldn't make a go of it, and sold his claim to a man named John Little who tried his hand at farming. John Little was more of a pioneer than a farmer, but he became romantically involved with a socialite named Elizabeth Livermore from Mill Valley, just north of San Francisco. Livermore fell in love with Big Sur and had a cabin built on a ridge south of the hot springs. In 1910, John Little sold his land to a doctor from Salinas named Henry Murphy – among other things he delivered a child who later became an author named John Steinbeck. Dr. Murphy built a simple hot springs retreat for his patients – the resort that Slate dreamed of. Even then, patrons had to travel from Monterey down to Murphy's Big Sur Hot Springs by a difficult carriage road, and lastly by horseback.

The passage down the rugged coast was treacherous…. It wasn't until the 1920s that a real road started to be built. An automobile road from Monterey to San Luis Obispo wasn't completed until 1937. From our point of view, in this nether world, Dick and I can watch it happening – watch how the road gets built.

As we watch – it's1933 and Jaime de Angulo, a doctor and linguist turned Big Sur Shaman, sits on horseback, up a ridge, overlooking the paving work done on top of the newly constructed Bixby Bridge (soon to be known as the informal "gateway" to Big Sur, where Jack Kerouac went crazy in 1962). Jaime de Angulo leans back in his saddle and takes a swig of wine from his leather bota. He mutters to himself, "¡Ahí va nuestro país!" (loosely translated: 'there goes the neighborhood'). What remains of the Nine disappears before his eyes....

Randell Jarrell, the poet, built a tower made of rock on the coast just north of Big Sur. As he watched that same scene unfolding he wrote, *"A horseman high alone as an eagle on the spur of the mountain / over Mirmas Canyon draws rein, looks down / At the bridge-builders, men, trucks, the power-shovels, the teeming / end of the new coast-road at the mountain's base. / He sees the loops of the road go northward, headland beyond / headland, into gray mist over Eraser's Point, / He shakes his fist and makes the gesture of wringing a chicken's / neck, scowls and rides higher."*

Like the enslavement of Esselen Indians, much of the dangerous road construction was done by prison inmates who were keep in camps along the coast. Tons of dynamite were exploded to cut a path across the ridges that ran down to the ocean. The destruction at Partington Canyon, where the Esselen tribe gathered acorns, was nearly absolute. Later, imagining Hiroshima, Big Sur natives likened what happened to a nuclear explosion. Many years passed before the oak forest returned. And with the new growth – with the new trees – came a batch of writers. Henry Miller moved into a cabin on Partington Ridge in the late 1940s. He was joined by Lillian Bos Ross who wrote novels about Big Sur pioneers – one called *The Stranger*. Her husband Harry Dick Ross helped the Fassetts, Bill and Lolly, build a designer restaurant called Nepenthe where Orson Welles and Rita Hayworth had once owned a cabin. Then Hunter S. Thompson moved into the old hot springs resort. Artists, authors, spiritualists and psychotherapists were the last strange wave to break over Esselen land before the ultimate corruption of Big Sur by wealthy Americans from Silicon Valley.

By the time the road was finished there were only two families that claimed to be related to the Esselen – one family in the northern part of Big Sur near the Salinas Valley and another in the interior near the old mission – at most a dozen souls. In a few years they were all gone. Some people in Big Sur tried to trace their ancestry to the Indians. But all that was really left of the Esselen was a potential human state of mind.

Then things started to change. In mid-October 1930, Richard "Dick" Price was born again in Chicago. Nobody knew that this was the Shaman who would bring the Nine back to Big Sur. His parents were merely human – moving the species toward extinction, along with all the others. How could they know who their son was?

Dick's birth, along with his twin brother Bobby, was by Caesarean. His family circle included his parents, Herman and Audrey Price, and there was a sister, Joan, who was born two years before. In 1933, in the fall, Bobby fell seriously ill with acute appendicitis, which initially was misdiagnosed. Bobby's appendix burst, causing peritonitis. An emergency operation to save his life was unsuccessful and Bobby died.

Dick felt left alone. Dick was only three – too young to understand Bobby's death. *"I kept looking for Bobby whenever I went to places where we played together. At some place inside, I held my mom, both of my parents, but more mom, responsible for Bobby's death."*

Dick came mostly under Audrey's parental influence and control. And Audrey became much more possessive of Dick. She turned Dick, in her own mind, into a kind of mirror image of herself. Herman seemed to withdraw into his business life. Socially, Herman became a charismatic figure, universally liked by business associates. He was strikingly handsome, intelligent – a focused man who was possessed by a huge work ethic – qualities that enabled him to rise from being a poor, non-English-speaking Jewish-Lithuanian immigrant, to a vice-president of the Sears & Roebuck Company. Herman was in charge of appliance manufacturing and became close friends with Raymond Lowry who designed sporty cars for Studebaker in nearby South Bend, Indiana. During WWII Herman was put in charge of manufacturing B-17 bombers for the Air Force, I suppose because a bomber is kind of like a big refrigerator. Herman was hardly spiritual. He had abandoned his mother's strict adherence to Orthodox Judaism and did not attend religious services.

Audrey, in contrast to her husband, emerged as a figure that was universally disliked by Herman's relatives. She was regarded as strong, hard, strict, rigid, cold, superstitious, overprotective, possessive, jealous, crazy, domineering, and controlling – you name it! She was into astrology. She used it to play the stock market. She became wealthy in her own right. In the Price family she was the dominant force, the tribal chief ... period.

In 1941, when Dick was ten, the family moved from their high-rise "penthouse" apartment near Lake Shore Drive in Chicago to Kenilworth, an affluent north-Chicago suburb. Their new home was a short walk from New Trier High School, which was one of the best schools in the country. But

Kenilworth did not allow for the sale of property to Jewish families. So Audrey coached her children not to tell anybody that their father was Jewish. She joined the Episcopalian church, and Dick and Joan were baptized. Audrey wanted the family to fit into the anti-Semitic neighborhood where they now lived.

In school, Dick was a good student and was surprisingly good at athletics, eventually going out for the wrestling team. Dick was not very big, a light-weight 5'10", but he was tough and very scrappy. He was a dominant high school wrestler who placed second in his weight class at the Illinois Wrestling Championship.

Dick graduated from New Trier High School in 1948. There was a lot of pressure for him to attend either Harvard or Yale, but Dick chose Stanford instead, because California appealed to him. Dick told me, *"I probably wanted to get as far away from my family as possible."* Leaving home felt like a liberating escape from the ruling power of his mother's authority and from a father Dick regarded as absent, uninterested and uncaring.

In the fall of 1948, Dick drove out west to Stanford University and started classes. Herman set him up with a brand new Studebaker and a bank account that automatically kept his balance at $1,000. Dick enjoyed a new sense of material and social freedom. His family may not have given him the kind of emotional support he needed, but they were certainly generous.

It was expected that he would complete college, serve in the military, and then pursue a career in business. As Dick said to me, *"My father had grown from an immigrant to a top executive. So, in some way, a little Oedipal I guess, my role in life was to beat what he was doing. So I had some image growing up that to consider myself a success I would have to be something like the president of U.S. Steel – right? – or president of General Motors!"*

Dick entered Stanford assuming that he would major in business. But the school didn't offer an undergraduate business major. So Dick began his college career studying economics – a subject that did not have a lot of interest for him. An introductory psychology course sparked his interest, and he changed his major. As Dick's interest in psychology solidified, he became a serious student, maintaining a 4.0 grade point average. He also developed a new career plan that he hoped could extricate him from the status-seeking type of life he associated with his parents. His new plan was to go to graduate school in psychology, become a psychologist, and eventually work as a professor or psychoanalyst. At Stanford he became a student of Gregory Bateson – the anthropological psychologist who developed the double-bind theory of schizophrenia. Dick earned his B.A. in Psychology from Stanford in 1952 and applied to Harvard University's newly created graduate program in social relations. He switched to Harvard that fall. As Dick described his situation to me: *"I wasn't interested in being an experimental psychologist. I was interested in, you know, if I had to label it in any way, in being a kind of anthropologist in mental health and illness, and it seemed to be a department where this might be possible to pursue."*

Harvard was a huge disappointment for Dick. He hoped that the department of social relations would be socially enlightened and less focused on experimental psychology, rats, and questionnaires. Instead, the initial course of study at Harvard directly focused on experimental psychology. He also found the department to be hierarchical, authoritarian, and filled with academic bickering. Toward the end of his first year, Dick wrote an examination paper that used the material he was learning to criticize what the department was doing. As a result, he got a "C," which was like getting a failing grade. The noted psychologist Henry Murray was the only professor in the department who showed any interest in helping Dick.

In the summer of 1953, Dick decided to leave Harvard. He told his parents he was going to transfer to either Stanford or the University of California at Berkeley. So he left *Cambridge Mass* for *California*! In the fall, Dick registered for some courses at UC Berkeley, including a course taught by a visiting psychology professor and humanistic psychotherapist Carl Rogers. Dick had read all of Roger's books as an undergraduate, but was unimpressed by the lectures.

Now Dick was feeling pretty much adrift. He decided to join the Air Force because a recruiter told him there was demand for psychology majors. He did his basic training in 1954 at Lackland Air Force Base. But instead of doing psychology work as he had hoped, Dick was given a job doing obsolete gunnery research. He was disappointed. For Dick the experience soon became *"a little like Harvard, I didn't get along too well with the people who were running things."*

Herman pulled strings in Washington, based on WWII connections from building bombers, and Dick was able to get a transfer to Parks Air Force Base in Pleasanton, California, where he worked as a teacher of recruits. It was good duty. His schedule was two days on – night duty for twelve to fourteen hours – then two days off. This meant he could go back to school. Both UC Berkeley and Stanford were only a half-hour away in his Studebaker.

In the spring of 1955, Dick started taking courses again at Stanford. One of the courses was taught by Frederic Spiegelberg – a popular professor at Stanford who was teaching a course on the Bhagavad Gita. Here's how Dick described the experience: *"For the first time, I began thinking there was something in religion; it was more than a system of deceit and enforcement of social rules."* At Spiegelberg's suggestion, he went to the Vedanata Society to hear a lecture by Swami Shokananda. Dick was impressed! Spiegelberg also recommended Alan Watts' lectures. Dick went and was *"immensely impressed; it was like nothing I'd ever touched into."* Alan Watts was on a weird trajectory from England – he recently resigned his job as Episcopalian priest in Chicago – and turned into a San Francisco Zen Guru. Watts profoundly affected Dick and he began taking courses at the Academy of Asian Studies where Watts was principal teacher. Dick took a room at the Academy and spent even more time in San Francisco studying Buddhism, meditation, and fraternizing with the new Beatnik scene that intrigued Alan Watts so much. Beat luminaries, like Gary Snyder, Jack Kerouac, Allen Ginsberg, and Lawrence Ferlinghetti, all attended Watts' lectures.

Dick began hanging out at The Place – a North Beach nightspot on upper Grant Avenue where he could get a pitcher of beer and find somebody interesting to talk to. At the same time Dick developed acquaintances with both Snyder and Ginsberg. And at The Place, he watched the transformation of the Beat scene as it burst into the national consciousness of the 1950s. Dick felt a sense of excitement and expansion.

Experiences he was having in his meditation practice were feeding Dick's excitement and expansiveness. At the Asian Academy he studied the writing of Nyanaponika Thera, the German-born Buddhist meditation teacher living in Sri Lanka. Dick incorporated what he learned into his blossoming meditation practice. He began having intense spiritual experiences, some of which excited him and some that were pretty disconcerting. Sensing that he needed some guidance, he went to his teachers at the Asian Academy and asked them what he should do. But teachers at the Academy were more like intellectuals than practitioners. They couldn't help him. He felt that the only people who could really relate to his experience were people who were involved in the Beat scene, like Gary Snyder.

This is how Dick explained what happened: *"Gary Snyder took me for a hike in Marin County north of the Golden Gate, up around Mount Tamalpais. The night before, we stayed at the home of Locke McCorkle and his wife Valery in Corte Madera, which was actually kind of a community. There was a party at Locke's house that night. Lawrence Ferlinghetti came up from City Lights Bookstore with Allen Ginsburg, Philip Whalen, Jack Kerouac, and even Alan Watts came.*

"That night Locke built a huge bonfire in the yard. It was a clear night with a full moon. In the warm glow people sat on logs around the fire. There was conversation and friendship. When the party was over Gary and I stretched out with mattresses and blankets on the floor of Locke's house. The next morning, at six a.m., Gary got up and cooked everybody a big breakfast. Then Gary and I slipped out and started walking down the road in the early-morning light.

"Gary was happy to be back in the wild. He said, 'The redwoods are beautiful here in Marin, so I'll show you Muir Woods today.' I walked behind him as we began to climb. We came to the end of a steep road, then across a high meadow, along another dirt road to the end, and then we followed a trail higher until we could see Corte Madera and Mill Valley far

away – even the top spires of the Golden Gate Bridge. Gary said, 'Tomorrow afternoon we'll hike to Stinson Beach and you'll see all of San Francisco – looks like Oz far away across the bay.'

"I told Gary, 'You know, back in town Alan Watts was saying to me that while people like us are excited to learn about Asians, actually the Asians are reading surrealism and Darwin.'

"Gary told me that East will meet West. He said, 'There will be a great world revolution when East meets West, and it will be people like Alan, you and me who start it.' ... 'See up ahead, such a beautiful mountain, such a beautiful shape to it, I really love Mount Tamalpais. We'll sleep around the other side tonight. ...Take us all afternoon to get there.'

"When we got to the end of a dirt road, we suddenly plunged into a dense redwood forest. We came up onto another road where there was a mountain lodge, then we crossed the road and went down through bushes to a trail, and we ended up in Muir Woods. It's a wide valley lined with towering redwoods. An old logging road led on for two miles – then Gary scrambled up a slope to a trail. We climbed up a steep slope and came out onto a highway and up the side of a hill and walked into an outdoor theater, classic Greek style, with the stone seats around a bare stone stage. We sat down and watched an imaginary

Greek drama from the upper stone seats. Far away we could see the Golden Gate Bridge and the splendor of San Francisco.

"Then Gary picked up his pack and started off again. In a half-hour we were at the Potrero Meadows camp. A few miles away we could see the lookout post on top of Tamalpais that looked straight down on us. We dropped our packs and spent a quiet afternoon lazing around in the sun. At dusk Gary lit a fire to cook a meal. We ate our supper. We were tired and happy. We washed out our dishes in the creek. A new moon flashed down through the pine trees. We put our sleeping bags down in the meadow grass and went to sleep early.

"During the night I had a vivid dream, one of the clearest dreams I ever had. I saw a Native American Shaman – he was standing just past my feet, looking down at me, studying me with an expressionless gaze. He was wiry, his face leathery hard and dark – red from the sun. His clothes were made of deer skin; he had a leather pack on his back. I woke up early, thinking: Wow, what was that about?

"I told Gary about the dream. He was already up building a fire and whistling. He said, 'Well don't just sit there, get up and get some water.' He got out a short-handle axe from his backpack and chopped some wood and got a fire going. There was mist in the trees and fog on the ground. Gary said, 'After breakfast, we'll take off up to the Laurel Dell camp. Then we'll hike the trail down to the ocean.'

"We had breakfast with fresh coffee brewed in a can from grounds. Then we started hiking along on the trail with Gary shouting back. 'Try the trail meditation – walk along looking down at the trail – don't look around – let yourself go into that dream as the ground moves by.'

"We arrived at Laurel Dell camp late morning – the surroundings were beautiful. Then at noon we started for the beach. We climbed up high on the meadow, where again we could see San Francisco far away, then we dipped down on a steep trail that fell straight down to the ocean. We hiked down the sea meadow to the beach, and walked out onto the sand. It was a foggy day with only occasional patches of sun shining on the beach. We stripped down to our shorts and jumped into the waves, but only briefly, because the water was cold, and we jumped right out again. Then I took a nap on the beach. After dozing awhile Gary got up and looked out toward the ocean and said, 'Look at all that water, stretching out past the horizon all the way to Japan.'

"We started back and went up the trail that had dropped us down to sea level – it was a hand-grasping climbing-hike among rocks and trees that exhausted us, but finally we came out on a beautiful meadow and saw San Francisco, once again, in the distance. That's when Gary said, 'Jack London used to hike these trails.' We continued along the south slope of the mountain with a view of the Golden Gate and Oakland miles *away. We trudged on for hours. Finally, we came down off the slope into a redwood forest, then up again, so steep that we were sweating. The last two miles we were bone tired. But soon enough we were climbing over the fence that led to a meadow looking over Locke McCorkle's house – right into the yard, walking the last twenty yards or so over fresh cut grass past a garden to the door of Locke's home."*

Then, after that hike, back in San Francisco, things started changing for Dick. A few months later – this was in December 1955 – a Beat friend named Gia-fu Feng came by the Academy to have dinner with Dick. Gia-fu was born in China but went to the Wharton School of Business in Philadelphia and then came to San Francisco as a teacher of T'ai Chi Chuan. Gia-fu introduce Dick to a woman he brought along to dinner. Her name was Bonita Fabbri. She was a beautiful Italian dancer who, like Dick, had grown up in Chicago. She was part of the Beat scene. Everybody called her "Bonnie" – a friend of Marilyn Chambers, one of Snyder's sweethearts that everybody called "Neuri." At the time, Dick was toying with the idea of becoming a Buddhist monk. Thoughts of a long-term relationship or marriage were a long way from Dick's mind.

As he was having dinner with Gia-fu and Bonita, he heard the disembodied voice of the Nine that said: *"There is your wife."* Dick looked up to see if anybody else in the room heard the voice. He started arguing with it sub-vocally, saying something like: *"Don't be ridiculous, I'm happy with the way my life is now."* …Within a couple months Dick married Bonita.

Dick and Bonita were married February 1956, in San Francisco at the Soto Zen Temple, in a ceremony performed by a Zen monk, Reverend Hodo Tobasi. The ceremony was conducted in Japanese with an English translator. The bridesmaid was Black, the best man was Japanese, and the guests were ethnically and culturally all mixed up. Dick's parents came out from Chicago, but to say the least, they were not very happy. Dick admitted to me that part of himself was deliberately trying to shock his parents. Dick described his experience at the wedding: *"My experience was very much like, hey, you know there's another me that's somehow vaster and greater, and there is the other Dick up at the altar being married by a Zen monk."*

After his parents left for Chicago, Dick and Bonita moved into an apartment together. He split up his time between Bonita and their life together, his job at the Air Force base, the Asian Academy, and the North Beach Beat scene. Dick's high-energy state made all of this activity possible. He was getting by on two hours sleep a night.

Dick was experiencing an upwelling of energy that he could barely contain. He was not having any problems at the base – a close friend was covering for him. Dick told me: *"At the time, especially with Bonnie catalyzing this, I started to go crazier and crazier. But in a way for me it was just this immense expansion and excitement which I was having trouble containing."*

On one of Dick's visits to North Beach, the huge state of internal energy he was riding burst through. Then, finally, one night in the Vesuvio Café – a bar next to the City Lights Bookstore in North Beach – all that energy came to a head. He felt a tremendous opening-up inside himself, like a fiery dawn. The bar had a fireplace. He thought it would be appropriate to light a fire in celebration of this mysterious event. He danced around the bar, chanting: *"Light the fire." ... "Light the fire."*

Instead of lighting a fire, the bartender called the cops and six large San Francisco policemen handcuffed Dick and wrestled him into a prisoner van.

After an initial detention at a medical facility in the Presidio, he was transferred to a hospital at Parks Air Force Base, where he was stationed. At Parks, he was given a couple of electroshock treatments and an occasional dose of Thorazine, but in general he appreciated the way he was treated. As Dick described it: *"For three months I was going through all sorts of experiences, some of which I remembered, some of which I didn't. One was a regression through history in which I felt like I was leaping through a series of past lives. Of particular importance was when the regression of lives came to a life with a Native American tribe where I was some kind of Shaman spending most of my time in meditation."* So, while in the hospital, Dick had what might be called, from a Zen perspective, a "satori" experience – an awakening in which he learned who he really was!

After about three months at the military hospital there was a major shift in his experience. Here's how Dick described it to me: *"I was in this balanced, fine energetic space and I remember my feeling was one of gratitude – to the nature of things and to my own nature. I was still a little volatile but I was no longer in the super excited state – instead I was in kind of a balanced state, a state that in some way I felt washed clean."*

He had passed through an experience that he would later call a "transitional psychosis" and he was ready to get back to his life and marriage. The Air Force was planning to release him from the hospital and give him an honorable discharge, despite the fact that he had another year and a half of his enlistment to serve. His preference was to *"get out as soon as I could. I wanted to stay on the West Coast; I didn't want to go back into my own family situation."*

Dick's discharge from the hospital at Parks Air Force Base never came through. Instead, he was notified that he was being transferred to another hospital. His father, by exerting his political influence through a high-level Air Force contact in Washington, got Dick transferred to an Air Force hospital in Illinois, about fifteen miles from the family home in Kenilworth. And then it happened. The "it" was a whole series of dishonest maneuvers by his parents that ended up getting him involuntary committed to the Institute for Living in Connecticut.

Dick's wife Bonita was taken back to the Price home in Kenilworth. But things didn't go very well between Bonita and her new mother-in-law. One weekend Audrey snuck into Bonita's room and found some letters. Audrey read some of them and convinced herself that Bonita was unfit to be her son's wife. When Dick found out – he blew up! For the first time in his life, Dick openly expressed anger to his mother. Dick moved Bonita out of the Price house. He returned to the hospital, and asked about getting his discharge. He wanted to get back to California.

Shortly after that, Dick's father came to visit the hospital and took Dick out for lunch to the top-floor restaurant at the swanky Marshall Field & Company department store in downtown Chicago. The table was covered with a freshly-pressed white linen table cloth. It was set with gold-trimmed china. They sat next to a panoramic window that looked down at the hordes of shoppers on State Street. Herman ordered prime rib and a split of Bordeaux. He plainly wanted to charm Dick – this was how he sold big clients on Sears appliances. During lunch Herman told Dick about a highly regarded private hospital on the East Coast, the Institute for Living, insisting that Dick should go there for a few months. *"What if I don't want to go?"* Dick asked. Herman told Dick … *"tough – young man, you go or I'll have you committed!"* So Dick agreed to cut a deal. He would go to the Institute for Living on a voluntary basis for three months.

Dick Price entered the Institute for Living on December 7, 1956. He spent the first few weeks in crowded, locked, smoke-filled hospital wards, unable to exercise or go outside. Given his voluntary status, Dick could – at least theoretically – sign himself out of the hospital and following a ten-day waiting period, get released. But when he tried to check out, the Institute notified his father, who had Dick committed with a bogus psychiatric diagnosis of paranoid schizophrenia. As soon as he was legally committed, Dick's parents had his marriage to Bonita annulled.

Over the next nine months Dick received fifty-nine insulin shock treatments, ten electroshock treatments, and large doses of Thorazine. His weight ballooned from 145 up to 240 pounds. He felt horrible. He decided that the Institute for Living was little more than a private prison in which he was being tortured. Dick seriously feared for his life.

Dick decided he had to escape. But he knew that in his overweight, physically weakened condition he simply was not capable of climbing over the hospital wall. First, he needed to get himself into better condition, despite what they were doing to him. To begin with, he learned to "cheek" the Thorazine pills they were giving him, rather than swallow them. But the electroshock treatments were taking a big physical and mental toll. The treatments felt like getting body-slammed in a wrestling match and getting knocked out cold, then waking up not knowing who or where you were. The insulin shock treatments were the worst. He would go into a coma and then he would wake up, unable to move because he was hypoglycemic. The only thing he could do to get some relief was to ask an orderly to give him some orange juice to raise his blood sugar. When he could move again, he would continuously walk the hospital halls, drinking large amounts of water. He began to wonder how many more treatments it would take to kill him. He thought he'd come very close to dying a couple of times already. Feeling desperate, he made up his mind that escape was his only option. They would not let him exercise. But he did his best to get into better shape, anyway, and he finally lost enough weight to make it over the wall.

It was a sunny August morning in 1957. Dick was dazed. He was an overweight young man in a hospital uniform shuffling down the streets of Hartford, Connecticut. He had just climbed over a wall in order to escape from the most expensive mental hospital in the United States. Dick told me, *"As I walked down the street in Hartford a single thought repeated itself over and over in my mind: Now what? I realized that I really did not have an answer."*

The first person Dick noticed was a bum sitting on the curb at a street corner under a tree… In fact, the bum was a Shaman sent by the Nine. Dick said hello, and the bum Shaman suggested they sit down together. It was a warm day and Dick felt better sitting in the shade instead of walking around without a plan. Dick figured out he could trust this Shaman bum, and talked all about his family and how they had tricked him into the mental hospital, then had him committed, then had his marriage annulled. Eventually he and the Shaman talked about what he should do next. In the process of talking Dick came to the realization that he was still too weak to make good his escape. Dick realized that the only way out of this horrible situation was to go back into the hospital temporarily.

The Shaman bum gave Dick some change to call his father from a pay phone. He made the call and told his father he had escaped but could not make it in the world. He said to his father, *"They've made me so ill, I literally have to recover my health. I'm not well enough to come out into a job or anything. I'm not even asking for you to get me out, now. I can't stay out, I may have escaped but I can't just go out there. I'm sick, now. I'm going to go back but I want you to get me on an open ward so I can regain my health."* Dick's father did what his son asked. Dick returned to the hospital. He was placed on an open ward and began the process of recovery.

Three months later, on Thanksgiving Day 1957, Dick was release from the hospital after a stay that lasted just short of a year. He was still weak. So he moved back in with his parents and took a job in the Chicago sign business run by his uncle Louis, as an assistant purchasing agent.

Working for his uncle was dull, but it allowed Dick to get his feet back on the ground. Then, after three long years of working for his uncle, he found out that Gia-fu Feng and some old friends were starting a cooperative living arrangement in San Francisco. It was called the East/West House. Dick decided it was time to go back to California and restart his life. His parents did not try to stop him. In May of 1960, Dick got on a United Airlines Boeing 707 jet airliner in Chicago that was headed for California. He knew what he was doing. Now he was a seeker. He explained to me that, *"My intention was to find a place where people who were going through the type of experience I had, could simply get better treatment, and to utilize whatever I might find to do that back out in California."*

Dick was able to re-connect with some of his mentors, like his Stanford professor Gregory Bateson and the British Zen philosopher, Alan Watts. They had long conversations. Alan was working on a manuscript that would later become a book with the title, "Psychotherapy East and West." Sitting in his office looking out of a bay window toward the Golden Gate,

Alan encouraged Dick to continue his meditation practice along with new forms of psychotherapy like Gestalt. These conversations made a big impression on Dick. …So much so that Dick was able to remember what Alan said.

Alan told Dick, *"You need to understand that both the liberation of Eastern contemplative traditions and the healing of Western psychotherapy – neither of which are particularly holy or complete – are aimed primarily at the transformation of consciousness. Eastern contemplative practice and Western psychotherapy – both of them – accomplish their goal through similar means. Namely, they aim at the deconstruction of social conditioning, the abandonment of dualistic grammar that implies a subject magically acting on some object, and the elimination of the pseudo-existential noun that gives us the false impression that things really are some **thing**.*

*"In other words, language and social identity trick us into thinking that things and individuals exist independently from other things and individuals. They don't! Liberation, healing and enlightenment come about with the realization that **that**

isn't true. This realization ultimately allows us to merge with our environment. As a new whole, we can see that what we used to think of as a separate thing is really linked with every other thing. Healing is just a way of becoming aware that already – right now – we are at one with the universe.

"We are released from the consensual trance of society and language – into the Gestalt – into the whole of the world – which results in a new playful attitude toward what I call – **this skin encapsulated ego**. We certainly don't cease to have an ego, but now we understand that our consciousness need not be essentially identified with this ego. We truly **have** an ego, and not the other way around. So we gain the ability to play at being a social self in the theatre of society, and not take the game of life so terribly seriously that it makes us sick. So, like I say Dick, don't take life so seriously...."

These conversations with Alan made Dick feel a lot better, as did his renewed friendship with Gia-fu Feng, the Chinese match-maker. Gia-fu was that Taoist businessman and sometime T'ai Chi practitioner who introduced Dick to new things – this time it was the text of the Tao Te Ching instead of a new wife. Dick discovered the Taoist resonance with Alan's teaching. In particular, Dick was taken by the eleventh verse of the Tao Te Ching, which Gia-fu translated for him this way: *"Thirty spokes support a wheel, but it is the hole at the center that allows the wheel to turn. It is not the clay the potter throws that gives the pot its usefulness, but the empty space within. Without a door the room cannot be entered, and without a window the room is dark. Such is the utility of emptiness."*

Dick had another important experience when he returned. It happened because LSD had not yet been declared illegal. In fact, in the early Sixties, LSD was being used successfully by psychiatrists to help traumatized patients unburden themselves. So, with the help of Gregory Bateson, Dick was able to do an LSD session at the office of a psychiatrist in San Francisco. Dick was able to experience a taste of the liberation that Alan talked about. As the experience of his "trip" progressed Dick started to feel a sense of expansiveness that had been ripped out of his life by the abuse he was subjected to in that Connecticut mental hospital. He regained a feeling of balance – the fine energetic state he remembered from the hospital at Parks Air Force Base. Just like then, after his LSD trip Dick said, *"I felt like I was washed clean."* And because of that experience, psychedelics became a life-long practice Dick used to find relief from the psychic scars left behind by abusive forms of psychiatry.

Also, back in San Francisco, Dick made a fateful new connection with another Stanford graduate – Michael Murphy. They had not known each other at Stanford, nonetheless the two of them ended up living next door to each other at the Cultural Integration Fellowship – a meditation center on Fulton Street. Dick told me: *"In retrospect it was almost as if I met up with a clone of my brother Bobby, because I rediscovered a little of what I lost when he died."*

Both young men had been influenced by the teachings of Eastern philosophic traditions and meditation practices. They had studied with and were influenced by Stanford Professor Frederic Spiegelberg and also Alan Watts. They had nonstandard experiences, both in 1956, leading to a rejection of the expectations of their families and society. For Dick, the experience was his hospitalization at the Institute for Living. For Mike, his experience was going to India for a stay in an ashram dedicated to a famous guru named Sri Aurobindo. After he returned from India, Mike Murphy quit his job as a custodian because his employer wanted him to work full time and that would have cut into his meditation time. So, finding himself free to experiment, Mike invited Dick to go down to his family's property in Big Sur. Of course, it was that same old hot springs resort that his grandfather, Dr. Henry Murphy, bought back in 1910.

The two friends loaded their possessions in an old Jeep pickup truck and drove south, down the coast from San Francisco. Their destination was Big Sur Hot Springs, a small resort now owned by Mike's widowed grandmother, Vinnie Murphy. Their intention was to start some kind of center for Eastern and Western learning. It was early 1962, just four years after Dick's release from the Institute for Living. Dick – the unwitting Ex'selen – the Shaman, accompanied by his new friend Michael, returned to the tribal home of the Esselen Indians. Dick became the co-founder with Mike of what they would later call the Esalen Institute. One of Dick's hopes for their new enterprise was that it would eventually become the kind of place where people who were going through difficult psychological experiences could find real help.

Dick explained this by saying: *"Mike just kind of mentioned to me that his grandmother had this old place down in Big Sur. Of course, I wasn't able to make any connection with my past life and the Esselen. It was something that only came to me later when I reconnected with the Nine. About that time I had been talking to a friend who was a psychiatrist who had himself been hospitalized. He had gone into psychiatry and we had talked about finding a place that would be more than the ordinary mental hospital. Michael's interest wasn't specifically in this area. He had spent over a year at the Aurobindo Ashram in India and his interests were more contemplative and intellectual. So we had originally talked about taking over the place as a conference center that would in some way apply itself to a range of interests: meditation, religion, extraordinary experiences, whether religious or psychotic."*

It was a time of change. There was a lot going on. Aldous Huxley died in 1963. Dick went to one of Huxley's lectures in Berkeley shortly after returning to California and remembered how he spoke about a new era when people would be able to explore what Huxley called the "human potentialities." The young men contacted Huxley about their project, and Huxley encouraged Dick and Mike from afar, but he didn't have time left to give them any direct help. However, after his death, Huxley's wife Laura and his protégé Gerald Heard both became supporters. Heard had tried a similar project in Southern California called Trabuco College, which ultimately was taken over by the Vedanta Society.

Also – about the same time – Nathaniel Owings, the genius architect, built an amazing home in Big Sur. Owings drafted an innovative Big Sur Land Use Plan designed to protect that unique coastal environment from the kind of destructive development that was endemic to California. Unfortunately, as we shall see later on, Owings efforts were undercut in the long run. But at least for the time being he kept the promise of "human potentialities" alive in Big Sur.

Dick and Michael took over the Big Sur property in October 1961. They co-founded the actual business that would become Esalen Institute in early 1962, and held their first seminars that same year. They were equal partners in the venture. Mike's family owned the property and Dick came up with the needed capital. …Dick negotiated a loan to capitalize the project. With some trepidation, he asked his father to release shares of stock they owned jointly. He used the shares as collateral for the loan. He was staking out new territory in his life.

The legacy crew that ran the place was a strange brew of personalities. The manager was a middle age woman – a Charismatic Christian who employed a group of temporarily sober converts to run the operation. The baths were occupied by militant gay men at night. David Murphy, Michael's older brother, who was a successful author, lived on the property. He had recently published a popular novel about an Army sergeant who had a secret crush on another enlisted man. It was critically acclaimed even by the likes of Henry Miller. So in short order David moved on – down to Los Angeles to work on screenplays. But there were other artistic influences. A very young Joan Baez lived on the grounds and could be heard practicing her protest songs in the early evening, as the sun set out there over the Pacific horizon. Emile White, who had been Henry Miller's close friend, lived on the grounds and published a travel guide for visitors to Big Sur. Later on, Emil built a memorial to Miller a short way up the coast highway. Miller, himself, had recently left Partington Ridge for Southern California. But there were others, like Hunter S. Thompson, who lived on the property and supposedly provided security between bouts of writing. He was emotionally attached to his Colt .45 Magnum pistol and his Dobermans dogs. The dogs eventually turned out to be useful for running off the gay men who occupied the baths. But Thompson threw an alcoholic fit, during which he used his .45 Magnum to shoot out the windows of the old Murphy house, for no apparent reason. And about that same time Thompson published an essay in a popular magazine describing the inhabitants of Big Sur in a less than complementary fashion. – *"Some are ranchers whose families have lived here for generations. Others are out-and-out bastards, who live in isolation because they can't live anywhere else. And a few are genuine deviates, who live here because nobody cares what they do as long as they keep to themselves."* That description turned out to be the last straw for Vinnie Murphy. She demanded Thompson's immediate dismissal. …So Dick had his work cut out for him.

Fortunately, Dick's Beat connections came back to help. Gia-fu Feng came down from San Francisco. He kept books for the business on his abacus. And the new enterprise slowly got off the ground. The idea of a humanistic retreat gradually gained momentum.

Dick explained: *"We started with the connections we had, through people like Alan Watts, and we began to set up programs. I think one of the first programs – it was probably early in 1962 – was Alan Watts. Alan did his own program from his own mailing list. At that time we tended to use people who had their own followings, their own mailing lists, their own programs, and we would just provide the place as a conference center for them. Then gradually, I think the following year, we began to get out our own catalog and formed Esalen as a separate entity. Before that we were running Big Sur Hot Springs, Incorporated, and then we started running weekends. We gradually got a few five-day programs, and otherwise we were running it for just drop-in traffic. Then gradually – I think by 1967 – we took the Big Sur Hot Springs sign down and put the Esalen sign up and attempted to make the whole place a conference center. The big turning point was the people who came in residence here – primarily Fritz Perls in 1964 and Will Schutz in 1967."*

A division of labor emerged between Mike and Dick. Mike took the more visible entrepreneurial role, lining-up the wealthy contributors and doing things for publicity. Dick took charge of the administration of the place itself – making reservations, doing housing, feeding the guests, keeping the business running and paying the staff and seminar leaders. He was really busy with running the place. In fact, Dick did not take a day off for the first eight years! Even then, he was still in recovery mode from quack psychiatry. So he would drop in and out of the seminars and workshops, when he had free time, hoping to find something useful for himself.

Differences in temperament took the co-founders in different directions as Esalen developed. Mike was uncomfortable in Big Sur. As a child, he felt like he had been dragged down the coast on boring vacations at his grandfather's rundown resort. He would have preferred playing golf with his classy friends in Pebble Beach. Because of this, Mike quickly moved away from Big Sur when he had the chance. But Dick, on the other hand, felt like he found his lost home. Unlike Mike,

Dick didn't put himself out in the public view, did not like to make speeches, did not go to conventions, did not flatter wealthy contributors from L.A., and did not like giving interviews to the media. But Mike was different. He teamed up with a Look Magazine editor named George Leonard, who had been sent from the New York headquarters out to California on assignment, and together they became Esalen's promoters in San Francisco.

So that's pretty much how Esalen got started. That's what Dick and Mike were about. That's how Dick Price landed back in Big Sur as Shaman at "the coming together of the three waters." That's an important aspect of the whole story. It's like, when you look down at the ground and see a rock. First you see the top of the rock. It looks interesting, so you pick it up and turn it over. You discover there's more to look at. And just like that, there's more of the story to tell. Which I guess brings up the next question. Namely, why is it me who's telling this story? Of course, that all depends…. It depends on me answering the question — how did I, Seymour Carter, end up at Esalen Institute?

You could say that I landed there as a refugee. In the early Sixties I was getting pretty strung out, living in Berkeley, with all that activism, the demonstrations and the drugs. I was bearded — long hair — everything. We were anarchists back then. I had been talking revolution for months — babbling night and day. Finally I got sent down to Big Sur by a comrade in order to chill out, because he couldn't handle me in Berkeley anymore. This comrade was a friend of Patrick Cassidy, a Beatnik refugee from the Bay Area who had a cabin in Big Sur. Patrick grew marijuana back in the hills. He was known as one of the Big Sur Heavies. He was tall and gaunt with a big black beard and hair down his back. Patrick was one of the original Gurdjieff spiritual influences at Esalen. He was a close friend of Dick Price. I would say that myself, Roland Hall, Dick, and Patrick Cassidy… We were the early 1960s players who were interested in consciousness, LSD experimentation, Gurdjieff thought, Buddhism, and yoga. Dick was the first person I ever met who did yoga. I would see Dick up on the road, running, and then I would see him down at the baths doing yoga.

So later on I got to know Dick and got involved with Esalen. I felt Dick's openness to me. I was very wild and maniacal at the time. What Dick did is something like what Meher Baba did in the 1960s. Dick heard about how Meher Baba collected all the craziest yogis in one place in India. Well, that's what he did at Esalen. Dick and Michael, both, gave refuge to the craziest characters of Sixties America. Eventually some of us over-did our stay. At some point, Dick would ask somebody to leave, or he'd "86" them or find a way to help them leave. If they wouldn't leave, he'd wrestle them out, send them packing. But fortunately for me, I ended up staying on at the magical Big Sur Esalen reservation as part of the tribe.

The geography of the place is kind of complicated. The Murphy property covers a few dozen acres of land between Highway One and the cliffs above the Pacific, divided roughly in half by a gorge where Hot Springs Creek empties into the ocean. Views of the property from the road are blocked by trees that stand along the top of the slope that runs down to the cliffs. On the property south of the creek, there's a steep entrance road about two hundred yards long that leads down to a guard shack where people check-in to the property. Just beyond the guard shack there's a large building — the Lodge — with reception area, offices, and open communal dining area with a big kitchen. The southern half of the property holds most of the housing for short-term visitors in several wings of what-used-to-be motel rooms. Scattered among these residences are converted meeting rooms generally named after luminaries — Maslow, Watts, Rolf and the like. Down a long path south of the Lodge there's the Bath House with multi-person concrete plunges wide-open and facing out over cliffs looking down to the Pacific. North of the gorge, across a footbridge, is the sprawling old Murphy residence called the Big House, with dramatic views of the ocean — it's generally used for longer-term workshops. Back across a grassy lawn, there's the Little House that served as Dick's residence, along with his family and guests. And north of that there's an assortment of structures, including an old barn that could be used for whatever was going on at the moment, and some marginal farm land that had been cultivated by John Little before the Murphy family took over. Underneath a raised highway bridge that spans the gorge there's a path that goes back into Hot Springs Canyon, where you can hike up steep slopes to the coastal ridge that turns into the Santa Lucia Mountains.

Early on — in the early 1960s — Abraham Maslow, the famous psychology professor who was the father of the humanistic psychology movement, just happened to be driving south along Highway One with his wife, heading down to L.A. It was dusk and Maslow was looking for a place to stay for the night when he saw the lights of the old resort flicker through the trees as he drove by. Maslow slowly drove down the steep entrance, parked and walked into the office. Gia-fu Feng was standing at the desk. He started to check-in the unexpected guest for an over-night stay. But when Gia-fu learned that this was none-other-than Abraham Maslow, he freaked out and ran back into the office. Dick came out with a copy of Maslow's new book, *Toward a Psychology of Being*. The result of this serendipitous encounter matured into a continuing commitment by Maslow to support this fledgling center for psychological enlightenment.

To sum up quickly — Dick was very far-sighted in his use of the property. He had been induced to see things in a certain way that was consistent with Maslow's mission because of the horrid treatment he had been subjected to by the medical psychiatric profession. It was this psychological disaster that gave him the drive to create Esalen as a healing place, with very skilled healers at these healing waters. He was very conscious of recreating something that was in the ancient Greek humanistic tradition. Dick was steeped in anthropology, psychology and a sense of human suffering, and his wrenching experiences opened up an abiding sense of compassion in him.

Esalen became a center of personal and social growth, and by 1968 Esalen was at the center of the cyclone of the youth rebellion. It was like Mecca for the Islamic culture. Esalen was a pilgrimage center for hundreds and thousands of disoriented youths interested in some sense of transcendence — breakthrough consciousness, LSD, the sexual revolution, encounter, being sensitive, finding your body, yoga. All of these things were first filtered into American culture through Esalen. By 1966, '67 and '68, Esalen had a worldwide impact. We were exploring all kinds of psychotherapy. The world's most important and pioneering minds in psychotherapy came and taught us. So we were like a convergence of cultural forces that never happened before. It was similar to the 1890s or 1920s in Paris, when there was a cultural convergence of people, characters, and cultural themes. Ways of being came together at Esalen and created this incredible three-ring circus.

Timothy Leary and Richard Alpert had been kicked out of Harvard for experimenting with LSD. They came to Esalen in 1962 looking for a place of refuge. So Dick gave them refuge; but they didn't take it for long — they left. Later, in about '67, Alpert came back from India as Baba Ram Das. Of course, Dick invited him to come and be a teacher and resident. So Ram Das was in residence giving Darshan talks every morning. But he came across as somewhat pretentious. He was from a privileged background, and he could talk a mile a minute, but he came up short when it was time for housekeeping. Patrick Cassidy said, "He's sitting closest to the stove but never chops wood," which was Patrick's way on nailing the character of this man. Big Sur was a place built on something more than pretense.

The Trotter men were Big Sur Heavies who measured up to Patrick's ideal. Frank and Walt Trotter were builders and backwoods men. Square and tough, they could build you a log cabin or cut a fire line with a bulldozer. Their father, Sam Trotter, was a pioneer. Sam came to Big Sur in the 1880s as a roughneck who worked at stripping the bark off tanoak trees in Partington Canyon. He'd haul the finished bundles of bark down to a little port precariously built into the cliffs of Partington Cove, where the tanbark was loaded onto boats for delivery to the tanning plants in San Francisco. Sam Trotter married one of the pioneer Pfeiffer-family women and settled down to build trails, roads, cabins and homes all along the mountainous coast of Big Sur.

But an even more important builder for Esalen was a man named Selig Morgenrath. He wasn't as physically daunting as the Trotters, but he was even more committed to structural integrity and environmental design. Selig was a Polish immigrant who was thrown into a concentration camp in New England because he refused to serve in the armed forces during World War II. Helen, his wife-to-be, was a student-activist who visited the camp. They got married after the war and embarked on a cross-country adventure that would lead them to Big Sur. They took a Greyhound bus from New York to Southern California; then they bought a car and drove north along Highway One. They stopped at Anderson Creek, just north of the Big Sur Hot Springs. There was a cluster of shacks that had been used to house the convict laborers who built the coast highway. At the time, Emil White, the self-made artist and Henry Miller's friend, lived in one of the cabins. Helen and Selig struck up a conversation with Emil and he talked them into staying. Helen and Selig lived at Anderson Creek for three years before moving just south of the Hot Springs to Livermore

Ledge, where Helen Livermore and John Little had built a cabin. The Morgenraths settled there and parented four children. They were living there when Big Sur Hot Springs started its transformation. Selig played a key role in building Esalen Institute. He became a close friend of Dick Price, and Dick immediately put him to work. Selig remodeled the buildings and grounds. He transformed old motel rooms into meeting rooms, remodeled the Lodge and the surrounding foliage. And then he helped to develop the work-scholar program that recruited candidates from around the world to come live and work at Esalen — cleaning the rooms, cooking the food and tending the grounds. Selig's no-bullshit approach and careful attention to details earned him the respect and friendship of Friz Perls, which was even more difficult to get than Patrick Cassidy's approval.

But Esalen, at the time, had a different kind of reputation in the outside world — different from the pioneer competence of these Big Sur builders. People made jokes about naked volleyball games at the Esalen "nudist colony," or they imagined everybody walked around with visible erections. Yes, Esalen had nudity. But the nudity was about authenticity. It was about owning your body. There was nudity on the lawn — a lot of groups were done in the nude. The baths, of course, were "clothing optional" but people generally didn't wear anything other than their point of view. For most of us, when we came down the driveway, it was a different world. It might be a cloudy day, and then the sun would come out. All of a sudden everybody on the lawn would just take off all their clothes.

It was a time when sexual boundaries, sexual limits, were relaxed. Esalen was kind of a breakthrough place in that regard. Those of us who were part of the resident community at that time were able to explore in ways that no one has since. It was a time of social explosion. Literally, you could walk onto the property, and in the next moment you might be down at the edge of the cliffs having sex within 15 minutes. That happened to me a couple times. And the baths were open to sex — lots of sex.

Dick was not as exuberant about sex, but he had his share. Jane Fonda was Dick Price's girlfriend in 1962, '63 and '64. When I first came to Esalen, I knew Dick was here, but I didn't see him much. But there was this pretty young woman wandering around. Someone said to me, *"Oh, that's Dick Price's girlfriend.... That's Jane Fonda."* I said, *"Oh? I've seen her in movies. She looks kind of scrawny to me in real life. She looks more 'ripe' in the movies."* Dick let me know that Jane Fonda had many virtues that I did not seem to understand.

To illustrate how it was at Esalen, I'll tell a story. It's about the resident Esalen psychotherapist, Fritz Perls, and his "circus" at Esalen. One day in 1968, two helicopters landed at Esalen on the lawn outside the Lodge. Out of one of the *helos* came Ravi Shankar, the sitar player, along with the Maharishi — Maharishi Mahesh Yogi. I was part of the group of people that brought Ravi Shankar to San Francisco for a concert, so I recognized him as he got out. And the guy coming out of the helicopter behind him was the Maharishi. Now, for those who don't know this, the Maharishi was The Beatles guru, and probably the most prominent and well-known guru at that time. During those times gurus used to appear like mushrooms after a rain.

So there I am — sitting and watching it all — and the whole crew at Esalen is watching it, too. Out of the next helicopter comes Ringo Starr and George Harrison. We thought, "Oh, wow. This is fucking amazing!"

Ravi Shankar and George Harrison go out on the lawn and start a sitar concert, and they gather about 50 or 60 people around them. We're sitting around listening to sitar music — and it's really nice. Then, the music ends…

There's a big rock at the end of the lawn. The Maharishi plants himself on top of this rock and is all covered with flower leis. He has stacks up to his ears of flower leis. They probably came from Hawaii or someplace. The Maharishi is sitting on this rock with a rug under him — very beatific looking and radiant. You know, like this radiant nut-job — that's how he looked. Anyway…he has flowers all over him, and flowers all around him, and he's sitting there on that stone. As the music ends he begins to lecture us about how love is everything. The answer to all life is to love everybody, according to the Maharishi. He's talking in a high pitched, strange voice. He just seemed about as awkward and as phony as anybody I had ever seen at Esalen.

At this time, Fritz Perls was about the most famous therapist in the world. He had a cameraman following him around who was making a documentary about Fritz Perls at Esalen. So, about the time that the Maharishi is fully into his pitch, and we're all being really attentive, we see Fritz Perls appear on the deck with a cameraman behind him. Fritz comes to the end of the deck, looks around, and puffs his cigarette (he smoked constantly).

Fritz would brook no rivalry at that time. Whoever showed up, Fritz would do something to make them look ridiculous, and to make himself stand out on top. He was "top dog" at Esalen. Every so often he would come around, and those of us who lived there knew that we're going to hear Fritz Perls say something — to lay a psycho-bomb on us that would drop us into bed for two days of introverted depression, because what he said was so heavy and so right-on. (Actually, I thought the guy was kind of a sadist. I mean, at times, he was just cruel. But whatever he said later turned out to be spot-on insight.)

So, there's Fritz, an old geezer in a red jump suit with a scraggly white beard, looking at this scene. I'm sitting in the audience. And I know that Fritz can't stand any competition. Clearly he's going to do something. What he was most famous for was reading body language. I remember many of his interventions being very acute — like, *"What are you doing with your hands."* The person he worked with would focus on their hands, and Fritz would say, *"Identify with your hands and express your existence."* Often, that would show that they might be talking sweetly about their mother, but they're actually making a fist, indicating deep-seated anger, which was the contradiction Fritz wanted to bring into awareness.

So...Fritz walks around the crowd with the cameraman following. Pretty soon he's got the audience split, like in a tennis match. The audience is watching him, and then they're going back to the Maharishi, then they're going back to Fritz.

The Maharishi's pitch starts to fall apart, and he starts speaking in a more and more high-pitched voice. Then his talk starts to stumble.

While our attention was divided like this, and the Maharishi is sitting there freaking out at Fritz stealing his show, the Maharishi actually starts tearing flowers apart with his hands in his lap. Fritz notices this and says very dramatically, *"Look at that fool, talking about love and kindness. Meanwhile he's tearing flowers to pieces."* Everybody is in awe. Fritz is playing the psychological executioner to the home crowd. It's so cool to see the Maharishi so masterfully deflated. As a result Fritz's reputation is secure, which is after all what really mattered to him!

Fritz was king baboon in our community. He was someone who was probably one of the world's great provocateurs — one of its great minds. We also had Gregory Bateson and we had Abraham Maslow and Joseph Campbell, and we had Will Schutz besides Fritz. We had all kinds of big-name people, as well as no-name people who were incredibly gifted. I would liken it to what the Bauhaus period was to art and architecture in Germany in the 1920s. At Esalen we were like that to psychotherapy and the new philosophy of the 1960s.

Will Schutz was Fritz Perls' main rival. Will was a big-shot psychologist with a national reputation for running training groups that broke through people's social barriers with straightforward interaction and extreme honesty. Michael Murphy pitched Will Schutz with the offer to make him "King of Esalen." He was awed by the iconoclastic atmosphere at Esalen and the physical attributes of young hippie chicks. Will finally succumbed. He was a barrel-chested, mostly bald, aggressive visionary, who took control of any group he walked into, which naturally set him up to be Fritz's main rival. Will ran Esalen's residential program — a half-year, all-out effort to explore new regions of human experience by resident "psychonauts," using meditation, encounter, sensory awareness, creativity, movement, emotional expression, inner imagery, dream work, peak-experience training, and the iconic Will Schutz brand of confrontational encounter. This program trained a series of outstanding group leaders like John Heider, and earned Esalen close attention from the news media. But a personality struggle was inevitable. It came to feature, but wasn't limited to, grand ego-battles between Fritz and Will and their followers for dominance of the Esalen community. For several years they maintained a rivalry from two poles of the property. On the south side there was Fritz living in a house that Dick and Mike built for him on a cliff overlooking the Pacific — and then Will working out of a house he rented for a nominal sum across the creek on the north side of the property. The strong personalities of these two leaders, living on the same isolated property, fueled an endless game of "capture the flag" — a shorthand term used by the tribe to describe the struggle for control of Esalen. There was no violence and very few verbal skirmishes — mostly just uncomfortable vibes in the Lodge at mealtime. There were no victors, except for Dick. Because finally Fritz moved to Canada to found his own training center and Will moved back to his cosmopolitan lifestyle of travel and television appearances. But for a while the sparks of transformative energy flew between these two masters and energized the atmosphere at Dick's tribal village.

And then there was also a dark side to the era. Good things weren't always taking place inside of people's heads and on the property, because we were diving into deep realms — with LSD, with psychotherapy, with the attitude that if you tell the truth and nothing but the truth everything will come out all right. I think we were like the French revolutionaries who were too insistent about the truth — and that didn't turn out so well for some people. Bringing the truth to certain people too early cracked them up. We had several suicides. Two or three people very close to me committed suicide. I think from that era of confrontation we were forcing intense self-examination on people who weren't ready for it. I feel that, yes, we had many failures in that sense. We did not get away without some really serious stuff happening. Then we had to back-off. I changed from *"you tell the truth all the time"* to *"you tell the truth that you want to tell now."* Tell what you feel safe in sharing with us right now. Keep to yourself what you don't feel like sharing. This allows for a range of expression.

There was one group in particular — the LSD group… It definitely brought about a breakthrough in consciousness. It gave an opening to everyone living in the stereotyped cliché world of America. Suddenly the gates of everything in the world opened wide. And that will go down in history as a time of people realizing that there's a lot more to subjectivity than we thought. There's a lot more — even — than what the religious traditions talk about.

But, as I say, there can be a dark side to having people do that much introspection. I think what we learned was that LSD needs to be used in the proper setting. This is what Leary and Alpert put together in the very beginning. Even though Leary said, "Take it all the time," he also said that setting is very important — and that's what we did at Esalen. Like with fire… Fire can be extremely dangerous. Many people are burned and destroyed by fire. But fire also has a positive element. To enter into our heavens and hells takes good guidance. It takes a proper setting….

I think that's what Dick's project was all about. He wanted, based on his experience, to put together a community of healers. Everyday therapeutic culture is focused on a one-to-one doctor/patient relationship. But you really need a community setting. That's what we tried to provide. It's the right kind of community setting that takes care of the dark side, and that's what Dick was up to at Esalen.

Stan Grof was also important at creating the proper setting. Stan was a psychiatrist from Prague. One day in the late 1950s Stan received a little box of capsules containing an experimental medicine from a Swiss pharmaceutical company named Sandoz. And that little box started a long strange trip that made Stan into the most experienced LSD researcher in the world. He ended up at John Hopkins hospital in Baltimore, doing a research project that experimented with giving LSD to borderline patients. When Mike Murphy heard about it, he made Stan an offer. And that's how Stan ended up living in Big Sur where — after LSD was criminalized — he was able to develop a new way of voyaging without drugs that he called *holotropic breathwork*. Because of the open atmosphere at Esalen, Stan was able to create a whole new form of psychotherapy.

So yes… Esalen had a very permissive bohemian atmosphere in its early days that led to surprising breakthroughs. And that permissiveness also allowed for new ways of relating. As a result, Dick — like most of the staff — had quite a few short-term relationships. One of Dick's liaisons was with a woman named Ilene Gregory, and that resulted in a son, David. But Gregory wasn't her real name — she changed it several times. She came from Back East — New Jersey, she said. She claimed that she got mixed up with the mob. Her husband was a crook. She left him. She was afraid that she was going to get killed. So she left Jersey and found refuge in Big Sur, working with the crew at the old hot springs resort. Dick kept her on and they became romantically involved. But she ran off, as she was disposed to do, and became involved with some kind of cult. Then Ilene came back with a son she claimed was

Dick's, and dropped off the child at Esalen — though by this time her relationship with Dick was long since over. It was not Dick's choice to have a child and he wasn't in a place mentally where he was able to be a parent. That changed over time. But initially the tribe took over as parent until Dick's attitude changed. The transformation happened with his second marriage to Christine Stewart and the birth of their daughter Jenny. ... So eventually, with time, Dick really was able to be there for his son. As David grew up, Ilene moved up to Napa — then changed her name again, remarried, and got stable enough to raise a child. But David would always come back to Esalen for extended stays that allowed him to establish a relationship with his father. And Dick was able to support his son, eventually to be whatever David wanted to become — which was *first* a professional musician in San Francisco ... then after Dick's death David served as general manager of Esalen and *then*, to everybody's surprise, he became a successful actor in Polish television and movie productions.

This process of learning how to be a parent was a difficult one for Dick. Throughout the 1960s, Dick still felt like he was in recovery from his own parents and from the Institute for Living. He was still in physical pain and he had a semi-constant state of restless internal energy that was at times very hard to manage.

Ida Rolf provided a partial solution. She came to Esalen in the mid-Sixties in order to help Fritz Perls deal with his health problems, which were enormous. Ida was a New Yorker who developed a unique cross between deep massage and osteopathy, punctuated by ideas gleaned from visits to Swami Muktananda's ashram in upstate New York. Her treatments were painful but dramatically successful in opening up and "restructuring" traumatized bodies. Fritz labored for years with intractable chest pain and complications from social abuse and chain smoking. Ida's ten session program of treatments gave Fritz temporary relief from the ailments that ultimately killed him. But in the process, Dick Price discovered the magic of what came to be called "Rolfing." Literally, Dick had hundreds of sessions, and ended up with a physique that displayed the muscular definition of a body builder!

But how much Dick suffered and how hard he worked on himself to maintain his psychological equilibrium was not fully appreciated by most of the people around him. Dick's three central practices were Buddhism, Gestalt and hiking. When agitated, he would often turn to one or a combination of these practices in order to help modulate his psychological state. And Dick's psychedelic "voyaging" — principally with LSD — also occupied a considerable amount of his free time. The hippie movement, that Esalen actually helped create, was in full swing in the late Sixties. It was populated mostly by drop-out middle-class kids who built illegal encampments back in the Hot Springs Canyon, especially during the summer months. They ensured that a variety of psychedelic drugs continued to be readily available, even though now declared illegal. With a reliable supply of high quality LSD, strenuous physical exercise, daylong hikes on the steep trails of the Ventana Wilderness, yoga, meditation, bodywork, soaking in the baths, the use of psychedelics and Gestalt work – all became the techniques Dick used for self-regulation, and were the tools he recommended for people working through their own psychological "states" or "experiences."

As a consequence, from the very beginning, Esalen was in a position to confront the issue of mental illness and how it was being defined and treated. One of Esalen's first seminars in the fall of 1962, led by Dick's old Stanford professor Gregory Bateson and psychologist Joe K. Adams, was entitled "Individual and Cultural Definitions of Reality." It grappled with altered mental states as well as alternative methods of treatment. Many more seminars addressing mental illness were to follow. By the mid-1960s, an alternative view of severe mental illness was beginning to emerge, and Esalen was one of the main forums supporting it. Perhaps the most eloquent spokesperson of the alternative view was the English psychiatrist R. D. Laing, who wrote about the possible value of psychotic experience. According to Laing, psychosis was *"a potentially natural process that we do not allow to happen."* He proposed the possibility that *"madness need not be all breakdown; it may also be breakthrough."* Psychosis can potentially be *"liberation and renewal as well as enslavement and existential death."* Both Michael Murphy and Dick Price were admirers of Laing's work, and they invited him to teach at Esalen in 1967. Of course, Laing was also a heavy drinker. He drank like a fish and ran up a huge bill at the bar in the Esalen Lodge, which he ignored. I actually remember holding a trash can for Laing to puck into one night. But we all have our moments. Dick was crazy sometimes, and I was always kind of wild…

In order to work on Laing's ideas, Dick welcomed a young researcher from the National Institute of Mental Health to Esalen named Julian Silverman. Dick wanted Esalen to sponsor a project in which psychiatric patients would be treated along the same lines that Laing had developed at Kingsley Hall in London — where psychiatric patients were given humanistic support rather than drugs or shock treatments and were allowed to work through psychotic episodes at their own pace. Julian had written an interesting article about Shamanism and the treatment of schizophrenia. It piqued Dick's interest. On a trip to the West Coast, Julian was invited to come down to Esalen for a visit. He was a slender, dark haired academic, dressed in black pants with a belt, black laced wing-tip shoes, and a short-sleeve white shirt. He walked into the Lodge, and just like Will Schutz, he was immediately impressed by the iconoclastic atmosphere and the physical attributes of the young women serving dinner. Julian was easily persuaded to take up residence at Esalen. In due course, Dick and Julian cooperated on developing what came to be known as the Agnews Project, a double-blind study co-sponsored by the NIMH, in which two groups of schizophrenic patients at Agnews Hospital near San Jose would be treated humanely, with one group receiving drugs, and the other a placebo. The results of the double-blind study provided solid evidence that schizophrenic patients who were treated without drugs showed more long-term improvement, better over-all functioning in the community after discharge, and lower rates of re-hospitalization than patients taking medication.

Dick hoped that the Agnews Project would eventually lead to acceptance of a mainstream alternative to the way severe mental illness was being treated in the United States. But, in the beginning, Dick did not realize that his involvement in the project would be supplemented by his own experience with another psychotic episode, just as the project was getting under way.

Dick's life in the late 1960s was incredibly intense. Mike Murphy left Big Sur to live in San Francisco in 1967. Dick had to manage the growing complexity of Esalen's Big Sur operations all by himself. He still hadn't taken a vacation — ever since Esalen opened. At the same time Jeanie McGowan, a woman Dick loved and lived with for two years, broke up with him. The pain of their breakup was something that stuck with him. All this stress drove him to work with, and ultimately train with, Fritz Perls. It was a turning point. And the process that unfolded ultimately led Dick back into his role as a Shaman.

Dick explained it this way: *"My interest in Gestalt came about as a direct result of Fritz Perls' presence at Esalen Institute. Michael Murphy and I started Esalen about two years before Fritz arrived. At first, Fritz came up from L.A., where he was working with Jim Simkin, merely to do a Gestalt program at Esalen. That was Christmas of 1963. But eventually he made Esalen his home, and we even helped him build a house on the property.*

"My initial reaction to Fritz was not very good. As it turned out, Fritz had just experienced a heart attack before he first came to Esalen, and apparently he thought he was going to die at any moment. Whether or not that was the reason, socially, he wasn't the most pleasant person to interact with, even when relatively healthy. So it took a couple of years — actually two years from the date of that first program — for me to start working with him. I started working with Fritz regularly in early 1966. The first time we worked together was probably between Christmas of 1965 and New Year's of 1966. I immediately became very impressed by what Fritz was doing,

and how different he was in a Gestalt group than my experience of him in regular conversation.

"What impressed me about his work in groups was that he was insightful. He was present. He was compassionate — all the things I didn't consider him as being when I would see him in the Esalen Lodge or around the property. I was very impressed that this man, a psychiatrist, was doing such good work compared to what I had experienced, and compared to what happens today with people who call themselves psychiatrists. As it turned out, Fritz was not qualified by the state of California to practice psychiatry. His German medical degree was not recognized. So what Fritz did at Esalen essentially defined a new category of practice. But it really isn't accurate to say that this practice is new, because Gestalt is as old as the world. It is a type of healing that is closer to so-called primitive societies, a process similar to a category of Shamanistic healing and ritual. That was its appeal to me. This approach was more humane. It came into contact with people

as real people, not as objects that need to be "fixed" in some way.

"In any event, I started working with Fritz in early 1966. Then I had my second mental break, which was largely the effect of not being able to finish the first one that I experienced thirteen years previously. So in the spring of 1969, I had another experience of a similar kind, most of which I was able to work through in Big Sur, but not at Esalen. I was actually staying with friends who had their own property, and who would protect the space for me to experience just what I was experiencing."

The break was probably *overdetermined*, as they say.... In late 1968, amidst all the intensity, Dick's father had shown up for a rare visit to Big Sur — the last visit before Herman's death the following year. Given Dick's family history, you can just about imagine how stressful that was. Dick and his father had an intense conversation in which, for the first time, Herman told Dick about his early life and the violence he had witnessed as a young Jewish boy in czarist-controlled Lithuania.

…Shocking… It seemed like this might explain, at least in part, Herman's behavior, his distancing and lack of emotional support as a parent. And it was after Herman left, in the midst of all the other stress, that Dick slowly began to edge toward a break. But this time he had advance warning and he took precautions to make sure he wouldn't be hospitalized and that his parents wouldn't find out.

Arrangements were made for Dick to stay at a remote cabin belonging to Patrick Cassidy, near Plaskett Ridge, south of Esalen. Being there, Dick hoped he could work through the crazy episode on his own, without psychiatric interference. But things were touch and go. Dick started sleeping at the foot of Patrick's bed, which also happened to be occupied by Patrick's new girlfriend. It became obvious that the episode wouldn't end quickly or smoothly. So Patrick brought Dick back to Esalen. After a short stay with his tribe, Dick moved to Jan Brewer's house in Sycamore Canyon, which was actually the old Pfeiffer house built on what used to be Pfeiffer homestead property. Jan Brewer was a Big Sur builder and real estate developer who had been subdividing the remains of the old Pfeiffer estate. In fact, Dick bought a parcel of the Sycamore Canyon property from Jan so he would have a place of his own to experiment and explore Big Sur. Later on, Jan got into some really bad trouble with drugs, guns and women, as the Big Sur real estate market turned into a play-thing for rich people, and Dick had to "86" Jan from Esalen. But in the meantime, Sycamore Canyon was a place the Esalen community used as a retreat, known to the tribe as the "blowout center." And during his second break, the old homestead was Dick's refuge.

While he was staying at the Preiffer house, Dick started to explore past lives. He entered the lives of several powerful historical figures. Two in particular… Alexander the Great and Napoleon Bonaparte. Here's how Dick described it to me: *"I would go in and out of awareness when I was in this state, still being completely out there but not having any recall and having a sense of coming to. So I would come to, finding myself striding up and down the 12-foot dinner table at Jan's place, being Buddha or somebody while everybody was eating. ... I was on a historical trajectory. ... So the way I remember it, first I was Alexander the Great, and when I got to Napoleon, I said: Forget it, this is ridiculous."*

Dick's experience was actually transformative. Becoming a figure like Alexander or Napoleon allowed him, in his mind, to reclaim what had been lost — to retake Big Sur for the Esselen. That had parallels to reclaiming his own psychological space, which had been plundered by misguided psychiatrists.

After several months of helping Dick reestablish his sense of personal autonomy, the friends at Jan Brewer's place who had been taking care of him were getting burned out. So with Dick's agreement they decided that he needed to finish up his experience as part of the Agnews project. Jack Downing, a psychiatrist and close person friend of Dick's, took responsibility for having him hospitalized at Agnews. Dick spent about ten days there before being released. He was housed on a ward in the hospital adjacent to the Agnews Project. ...To the staff's surprise — here was the person who actually had been instrumental in creating the project in the first place!

After his discharge from Agnews, Dick traveled to Canada with Julian Silverman to take part in Fritz Perls' first Gestalt training session at a new center, the Gestalt Institute of Canada, on Lake Cowichan in British Colombia. He was able to work with Fritz on the things he experienced during his break. Then, at the close of training, Fritz Perls announced that Dick had fully "recovered" and was ready to start leading Gestalt groups and trainings at Esalen Institute.

Dick explained what happened like this, *"After I got finished with my second break, which was in the summer of 1969, Fritz was already preparing to re-locate himself. He left Esalen after six years, and re-established himself at the Gestalt Institute of Canada at Adelaide College on Vancouver Island. I went up there and spent two of his last three teaching months with Fritz in Canada. There was a training institute that had been established there. At the end of the training, that's when Fritz said to me, 'Dick it's time for you to go out and teach. Do your own groups.' So in late 1969 I left Canada and came back to Esalen to start teaching Gestalt. Just after that, Fritz left*

Canada and went on a tour of Europe for the winter. He got sick in Europe, and then sicker still when he got back to the U.S. He never made it to Canada. He died in Chicago in March of 1970. So that's when I started teaching Gestalt Practice — when I got back to Esalen in 1970."

Returning home from his second break and his trip to Canada, Dick began to put more and more energy into Gestalt work. He led Gestalt seminars at Esalen, ran Gestalt training programs, and worked as a Gestalt facilitator with Esalen's visitors and staff. Dick continued to champion the rights of mental patients and extended himself to anyone in the Esalen community who was in psychological difficulty. He supported many people going through psychotic experiences at Esalen — people who, he admitted to me, *"otherwise would have been locked up."*

Both because of, and in spite of, his painful experiences in mental hospitals, Dick embarked on a lifelong journey of intense personal exploration. Dick's searching involved two rare trips away from his Esalen home. The first was his participation in Oscar Ichazo's Arica One training — a form of Gurdjieffian Sufism — in New York in 1971. The other was a trip to Poona, India to study at Bhagwan Rajneesh's ashram in the late 1970s. Both Oscar Ichazo and Rajneesh held out the promise enlightenment. They both offered a combination of psychological, spiritual, and physical practices that Dick had, for years, been attempting to synthesize himself. Both tried to use Dick and his position as co-founder of Esalen for their own proselytizing purposes. In the end, what Dick found most troubling with both Arica and Rajneesh was that *"everything you try to do that is a variance with the company line, is ego. So you're already categorized, there's no way to come back at it. The only way to come back at it is to quit. Which I did, both at the Arica training and with Rajneesh."*

Following Dick's experience with Arica and Rajneesh he stopped looking for something outside himself. He finally rediscovered the Nine — that constellation of supra-human entities from the star Sirius. Jenny O'Conner, an English psychic, channeled the Nine for Dick at Esalen. Initially, they gave him information about his hospitalizations that he had never heard from anyone, and they helped him make sense out of some of his strangest experiences.

Working with the Nine was something, in his last years, where Dick didn't have the feeling anymore of, *"I'm looking for what is bigger than me so I can feel held."* He came to another kind of understanding of his own inner practice as a place where it could serve something greater. The Nine reminded Dick that he was Shaman, the leader of a tribe. And he came to understand that the tribe could serve the Nine, with all the inevitable limitations of a human collective, even as the Nine served the tribe. As a result, Dick came to a certain maturity where he wasn't looking for anything outside his tribe anymore.

Now that Dick reconnected with the Nine he was able to contact their awareness, especially on long hikes — excursions with his dog Aurora back into the Santa Lucia Mountains. Aurora was a large white canine with the stamina needed to match Dick's energy on the trail. Back in the mountains, sometimes on multi-day journeys accompanied only by Aurora, the Nine showed Dick the shape of a future species with the kind of awareness that Dick had worked to bring back into Big Sur.

Dick maintained his scan of the spiritual/psychological horizon. He embraced this along what he called *"the psychological-spiritual front."* This last exploration was what he called his *"research project into paranormal intelligence."* Dick worked with Jenny O'Conner through automatic writing by which she was able to channel the Nine — now fully identified as supra-human. Dick used the Nine as paranormal management consultants who helped him run the Esalen community. They also occasionally served in the role of Gestalt facilitators. Dick would ask the Nine a question and they would respond through Jenny's automatic writing. In this way the Nine would give Dick psychic insight into how Esalen might actually improve its operations. But there was resistance. Around Esalen the authority of the Nine was not universally accepted. In the community the Nine were much better known for performing the role of extraterrestrial hatchet men. But, if nothing else, the Nine provided Dick with an opportunity to express a different aspect of himself as a manager — the mischievous Shamanic trickster in him — to keep everybody guessing. It was a role Dick enjoyed and became infamous for.

Early in 1982, a key moment happened in Dick's relationship with the Nine. It came at the time when Dick asked the Nine about his own dream for the world. He asked the Nine, *"And how do you see the place you hold in my dream?"* The Nine responded, *"In transition to await the next move,"* Dick asked back, *"And how do you see my role in that transition?"* They answered, *"As always, our dear worker in the world, as facilitator."*

Eventually the Nine were listed in the Esalen catalog of programs, where they were identified as program leaders. They were also listed as members of the Esalen Gestalt staff, along with Aurora. And, in fact, the Nine recommended that Aurora should be nominated Chairperson of Esalen Institute's Board of

Directors. But when asked, Aurora declined the honor with a subdued growl.

Despite the importance of the Nine, what Dick found most useful was his exploration of many forms of psychotherapy, personal growth and spiritual practice, utilized both personally and as part of his new form of Gestalt Practice. Whatever was life affirming, he used. Whatever he found to be coercive or demeaning inevitably was something he rejected.

Gradually, Dick Price came into his own during the 1970s. And one of the major contributing factors was his second marriage, this time to a precocious young woman named Christine Stewart. Dick met Chris in February of 1971, when she came out from Washington, D.C. to attend a Gestalt and Rolfing workshop that Dick co-led with Hector Prestera. Chris returned to Esalen in the fall of 1971. That's when she and Dick became romantically involved. In October of 1972, Chris decided to live at Esalen permanently. They married in February of 1974 and had a daughter — Jennifer — late in that same year.

Dick's marriage to Chris and the birth of his daughter had a profound positive impact on his life — something everyone who knew Dick was in agreement about. He was so deeply insulted by misguided psychiatry that it was clear he needed a trustworthy loving relationship. Then Chris came into his life. Chris turned out to be a complimentary influence for the Nine in the sense that she was a very beautiful woman, loved Dick unrestrainedly, was a nurturing soul-mate, and a genuinely warm person — all those things that Dick needed in his life.

Dick's relationship with his daughter Jenny turned out to be transformative, eventually helping to take the sting out of his painful past. He had been through incredibly bitter and hard feeling times with his own parents. It was a long siege between him and the past. But he wasn't in that state those last couple of years. When Jenny was born it made a difference and it kept making a difference. Dick reworked many of his relationships just from being a father. His relationship with his son David became deeper and more intimate. Dick's marriage and his relationship with his family enabled him to begin to feel a sense of contentment with his life, and he began to trust that life had the potential to be satisfying.

Another form of transformation for Dick was the development, together with Chris, of his own new form of Gestalt work. Though their work was similar to what Fritz did, Dick and Chris came to emphasize different aspects of experience as he changed what he had assimilated from his mentor into a style more in keeping with his own personal experience.

Dick specifically chose the term Gestalt Practice in order to separate what he did from more traditional forms of psychotherapy, including Fritz's authoritative doctor/patient style of Gestalt therapy. This is how he explained it to me:

"In Gestalt Practice the authority to make choices remains with what we call the initiator. It's quite different from patient/therapist roles. The initiator designates an active role, while the word "patient" implies, at least to me, someone who lies back and is acted on. The role of the doctor is for me the one who acts. Therapy is active. Practice isn't something the

therapist does to a patient. It's what two people in complementary roles do together."

Dick was a very body-based person. So Wilhelm Reich's body-based therapy was an important influence on him. Dick put direct focus on the body in his Gestalt work by paying attention to breath and bodily sensations. His concept of *"basic practice,"* which he defined as *"becoming established in body and breath,"* was the way he began many of his Gestalt sessions. And it was a place he returned to, for grounding throughout his sessions.

Basic practice consisted of attention to breath, to movement, to kinesthetic sensations, to sensations in the body — feeling states, emotion, thought, images. What was important for Dick was the mode of present-centered contact that didn't judge the content of what came up in a session. This is how Dick described what he did: *"Gestalt, as I practiced it, was fundamentally the same as what I learned from Fritz, except that I made some changes. Fritz made a strong point of not wanting disciples. As he put it, 'I do not want to train a lot of* little Fritzes.' So what I got from Fritz, I put into my own wine bottle, so to speak.

"Gestalt is a German word that means configuration. Of course, nothing is ever perfectly defined. I asked a German guy in one of my groups what the word meant, and he defined it as figure. It's like saying that there's a bridge over there, and you see the shadow of a man passing over it, but you don't see him clearly. When you see the figure, you are seeing a Gestalt. It's an impression of the whole. But it doesn't necessarily have to have a lot of clarity or detail. You don't have to see the man's eyes, or the way he buttons his shirt. You just see the figure — the configuration — in the sense of the verb to configure.

"Fritz and Laura Perls came from Berlin. At the time, Laura, especially, was in contact with the various Gestalt psychologists who eventually left Germany — most of them Jews. Many of them, like Kofka, Kohler, and Wertheimer, ended up teaching at the New School for Social Research in New York during the early 1930s. They were doing experimental work, mostly with perceptual wholes. For example, you might see a *single image in different configurations. In one particular perceptual experience, you might see a configuration that would look to you like two faces kissing. In another instance, you might see the configuration as a vase. Gestalt psychologists were working, mostly experimentally, in relation to these intriguing problems of perception. However, in what became Gestalt therapy, and then Gestalt Practice, we were interested in wholes, but not just as perceptual figures. In Gestalt Practice, the whole would include a perceptual element, a feeling element, and a sensational element. The total Gestalt, rather than merely a perceptual figure, might include an emotional figure, as in, 'Now I'm feeling sadness,' or a sensual figure, 'Now I'm feeling a pain in my forehead.' There was the ability of the perceiver to choose and to come into relationship with a field of experience in a way that could lead to greater and greater satisfaction. One simple example is to say, 'Oh, now I'm hungry.' With this awareness there is the discovery of, 'Now I have the ability to choose.' I can open the refrigerator and eat something, and then I'm no longer hungry. So we were always looking at this ability to form Gestalts, and then at letting go of Gestalts, in relationship to organic self-regulation. So that's essentially what Gestalt is about — regulation both in an individual sense, and in a larger sense of social fields.*

"In order for me to describe how I did Gestalt Practice, I actually have to talk about what I didn't do, because Gestalt is not a 'doing.' What Fritz called therapist and patient, that dyad, I refer to as reflector and initiator. The initiator is really the person who formerly was in the 'patient' role. My function was simply to be available in a particular way to reflect and clarify whatever comes up in that person's process. I never defined how a person should be. I was available in a particular way, like a mirror — which is a good analogy. So the person remained responsible for his or her own experience. This was very unlike the standard psychiatric approach — where you are put, if not in a jail cell, then certainly in a diagnostic pigeon hole of symptoms.

"The central form that my work took was the 'open seat' group. In order to describe what happened, let's say that there *is a group of fifteen people sitting in a circle. There are some basic awareness exercises that I gave to the group. This is what I called basic practice, which is attention to the body, to breath, to movement, to kinesthetic sensations, to sensations in the body — feeling states, emotion, thought, and images. And what's important is a mode of present centered contact that is brought to the experience, without judgment. So what's important and basic in the practice isn't about change. I was not trying to change anyone. What's important was contact. I functioned as an auxiliary to encourage and facilitate contact — that is, contact with one's own experience, not defined by anyone else from outside.*

"*After the basic practice exercises, the opportunity was there for people to join me on the open seat — or not. The choice remained open. The authority to make the choice remained with what we called the initiator. It's quite different from psychiatry. The word "initiator" designates an active role, while the word "patient" is someone who, at least to me, is acted upon — and the therapist is the one who acts. Process is different. Process is active. So my Gestalt wasn't 'therapy.' It was a 'practice.' It wasn't something that a therapist did to a patient. It was what two people, in complementary roles, did together."*

Dick's Gestalt work became his central practice — a practice that was strongly aligned with his long-standing interests in Buddhism and meditation. Unlike Fritz Perls' dramatic Gestalt style, Dick's Gestalt work was meditative, focusing primarily on the quality of awareness brought to moment-to-moment experience. Dick was doing an ongoing spiritual practice that served both himself and the people he worked with.

The depth of Dick's spiritual practice was obvious when he conducted Gestalt sessions. The source was his direct experience of the spiritual dimension of consciousness, combined with his deep interest in other people — in who they were — without any need to reshape them to fit his world view or notions of what should be "real" or "true." This spiritual dimension evoked a deep feeling of acceptance in the people that Dick worked with.

Dick encouraged others at Esalen to live lives of intense psychological and spiritual exploration. For many psychiatric survivors, Dick became a role model for what they could hope to model and achieve — namely, a successful, satisfying, independent life without the use of mind-numbing medication. This achievement was also a culmination.

On November 25, 1985, following a day of intermittent rain, Dick decided to take advantage of a break in the weather for a quick hike up Hot Springs Canyon. His destination was "the source," the site where Esalen's water supply was taken from Hot Springs Creek. Dick did not plan to be gone for very long because he had business meetings scheduled that afternoon. But it turned out to be Dick's last hike.

A forest fire in the mountains behind Esalen — the Rat Creek fire — had burned down the ridge the previous summer and left Hot Springs Canyon nearly bare of vegetation. In the fire's aftermath, dislodged rocks started rolling down the hillside, breaking Esalen's water line. When the rainy season came, silt and sediment flowed into the creek clogging the catch basin and cutting off Esalen's water supply. So Dick made it a point to routinely check the water line and the catch basin at "the source."

On that Sunday, a boulder about the size of a small car was dislodged from the steep, rain-soaked hillside of Hot Springs Canyon. From high above "the source" this boulder fell toward the canyon bottom. Dick was surprised by the loud noise of the boulder crashing downhill. The boulder split apart when it hit the creek. One of the pieces flew up and hit Dick in the head, breaking his neck. His body was found in a seated position in the shallow water that drained out into Hot Springs Creek from the overflow channel of the catch basin. The top three boards that formed the dam for the catch basin had been removed. One of the boards was found under Dick's body. The lower two boards were smashed and broken by the piece of the boulder that had killed Dick. So he had been in the process of cleaning silt from the catch basin when he became aware of the sound of the falling boulder as it crashed down toward the canyon bottom, ending when it shattered as it hit the creek. A fragment flew through the air. It struck Dick and killed him instantly.

That evening, when Dick had not returned from his hike, Brian Lyke, the operations manager of Esalen at the time, organized a group to search up the canyon. They found Dick's body and carried him back down to the Little House. Dick's death was so sudden and so unexpected that it threw the Esalen community into turmoil.

In this awareness space where we are now, watching from above, we can see the scene in the Little House, looking down at Dick's body lying dead on his bed, framed by a background of California holly bushes outside the window — the bushes heavy with bright red fruit. We can see the feelings in the room. We can see the emptiness. Everybody feels like they are lost. Dick's friends feel lost. Dick's wife Chris and his daughter Jenny feel lost. And we can see how Esalen is lost.

But here and now, together with Dick again, as we move out of the world, we can see that nothing was really lost at all.

There was peace in Dick. There was completion in Dick's life. His work in the world was over. At a time when it appeared that Esalen and Big Sur were cut loose to drift toward an uncertain fate without him — that same thing had happened centuries before.

So much of what Dick wanted Esalen to become and to contribute to the world proved unsustainable without his presence. And that serves as a reminder of just how fragile the condition of the human species is in the world. After Dick's death Esalen entered a gradual decline. Chris Price stayed at Esalen for a couple of years — until the place started to change. Esalen's new management had different objectives. Chris left, and with that, the Nine began to lose interest.

Long before Dick's death Mike Murphy had returned to the San Francisco Bay Area. Up there he was able to write a quasi-spiritual novel about golf. It was a success and he was finally able to compare himself favorably in his mind with his brother. Then he tried to run an outpost office of Esalen in the city — on Union Street close to the Gestalt Institute. But it was a financial disaster and a drag on the Big Sur operation. It had to be shut down. Then Mike got involved with a group of Russian psychics and eventually he set up an exchange program that even hosted Boris Yeltsen — the soon-to-be Russian president — who came to the United States on an alcoholic post-Soviet tour. Esalen appeared to prosper once again under the influence of privilege and money. Mike ran an invitational program of seminars down in Big Sur that imagined a new kind of life-after-death in a new kind of spiritual body. And the old hot springs resort got remodeled for tourists, for entertainment types from Hollywood, and for wealthy entrepreneurs from Silicon Valley.

As Big Sur appeared to fall under the spell of money and tourism, Ansel Adams, the famous nature photographer who lived in Carmel — along with Nathaniel Owings' second wife Margaret Wentworth Owings — led an influential group of environmentalists who tried to get the federal government to regulate the landscape of Big Sur, kind of like what was done north of San Francisco with the Point Reyes National Seashore.

Leon Panetta, in Congress at the time, introduced legislation that would have preserved Big Sur. But rich property owners opposed it. Some people affiliated with Esalen, who were sympathetic to property interests, encouraged Senator S. I. Hayakawa to kill the legislation. Then in early 1986, shortly after Dick's death, Monterey County finalized a land use plan that protected the scenery of Big Sur, but also protected wealthy landowners. Property values skyrocketed. Socially, the community got divided between wealthy property owners and tourists on one side of the American economic divide, and minority service providers who mostly had to commute up to Monterey to find affordable housing on the other. The scenery of Big Sur was preserved as a breathtakingly beautiful attraction for tourist and wealthy Americans. And the Nine became even more disgusted with the human species, watching as we collectively grovel toward extinction.

From our perspective now, after leaving human embodiment, Dick and I can see this for what it is. It's what happens to humans, individually and generally. Humans automatically head for the trap of individual privilege and greed, and in the process we destroy our world.

So with Dick's death the Nine turned their attention to a successor species. And as the consciousness of these new beings take hold, a few generations of humans remain behind. Humans become the new Neanderthals. And just like Neanderthals when humans first showed up, some of us stick around for a while, as we gradually get replaced by a new species with greater awareness.

And that's okay... That's the plan... That's the dream... Here... Now... Everywhere from our perspective... As we look back... As we move out into the perpetual dawn of the Universe.

Printed in Great Britain
by Amazon